CLASH OF THE TOTEMS AND THE LOST MAGAECIANS

CLASH OF THE TOTEMS AND THE LOST MAGAECIANS
BOOK 1

Yonnie Garber

Matador
Unit E2 Airfield Business Park,
Harrison Road, Market Harborough,
Leicestershire. LE16 7UL
Tel: 0116 2792299
Email: books@troubador.co.uk
Web: www.troubador.co.uk/matador
Twitter: @matadorbooks

ISBN 978 1803131 146

British Library Cataloguing in Publication Data.
A catalogue record for this book is available from the British Library.

Printed and bound by CPI Group (UK) Ltd, Croydon, CR0 4YY
Typeset in 11pt Baskerville by Troubador Publishing Ltd, Leicester, UK

Matador is an imprint of Troubador Publishing Ltd

To Keith who reads all my stories

CONTENTS

1

BURN DOWN THE SCHOOLS

Mum was waiting anxiously for me inside the school gates of Saint Timothy's, a small private school in a village called Tribourne. I got out late as Mrs Hooker (unfortunate name for a teacher) held me behind with my best friend, Letty Keel, to reprimand us for acting *inappropriately*. That teacher had no sense of humour. She said we weren't taking our music lesson seriously, but I burped in perfect time and pitch to Beethoven's Fifth. What was the problem?

"Have a good weekend," shouted Letty as she spotted Billy Carlisle waiting for her outside school. "I'll call you. Maybe we can meet up and do something." Letty was tall with golden hair that curled at the ends. I, on the other hand, was told by the local baker last week that I was a *little cutie*, which was a compliment for a six-year-old but not for someone twice that age and about to become a teenager in a couple of days.

"Sure," I called out to her but she'd already disappeared off with Billy.

"A bit young for all that, don't you think?"

"Mum…it's not like that! Anyway…you don't understand today's kids." Before I had a chance to continue my lecture on how mature the kids of today were in comparison to her day, she handed me a Tupperware box.

"Pick some wild blackberries on your way home for tonight, won't you, please, Ellery? I've got a staff meeting here…shouldn't be more than an hour."

I took the box from her.

"…and take *him* with you." She gestured in Thomas Marks's sniffling direction, who was putting his phone back into his chocolatey pocket and wiping his eyes with his blazer sleeve.

"What's up, Thomas?" I asked, bending down to him as he sat slouching his large frame against the low wall. His red chubby cheeks seemed to continue straight into his neck. They looked like a couple of freckled pouches. If it wasn't for his size, it would have been hard to believe he was in the same year group as me.

"He's forgotten. He always forgets when it's his turn to have me."

"Your dad?" I guessed. It seemed pretty obvious that collecting Thomas from school was quite low down on his dad's list of things to remember.

Thomas nodded, putting his hand back into his pocket to retrieve some of his melted chocolate raisins. "He said he lost track of time while out shopping with Naomi. Mum hates Naomi. She says she looks like a sixth-former. I give up. How am I going to get home now? Dad's in London and doesn't want to leave, and Mum doesn't get back from work for two hours. I've missed the last bus."

"You can come back with me. It's only a short walk. Besides, you can help me pick wild blackberries along the way. They're my dessert tonight." I handed him the small white Tupperware box. Thomas stared bewildered back at me. Most kids at Saint Timothy's thought that money grew on trees, and fruit and veg grew magically on supermarket shelves. Most of my class thought my mum and I were weird. *We* weren't weird – *Mum* was weird. We didn't even own a car as it was *bad for the environment*. All my friends' parents didn't just own *one* car but multiple vehicles in multiple colours. One girl's dad had a private jet. Then, of course, there was Mum's issue with meat. We weren't exactly vegetarians but we didn't eat a lot of meat, only on special occasions. Mum could be so intense sometimes. Her late brother was a vegan and very eco-friendly, so it was her testament to his memory. Boring! If she only knew the number of times I'd eaten burgers and chips at school, she'd have a fit.

"Is your mum really going to introduce *meat-free Mondays* at school?" asked Thomas, staring into the Tupperware box.

I didn't answer, thinking only of the possibility of losing even more friends from the very few I already had if she did.

"Irene Sturrage says your mum's a witch," he added.

"Well, Irene Sturrage is an undersized know-it-all with the brain the size of a pickled onion. Mum likes experimenting with herbal remedies…that's all." I stopped for a minute, remembering one of her remedies for a sore throat, which turned out to be as appealing as a bowl of dog sick.

3

"Irene says your mum turns kids into frogs and that you've got no dad because she must've killed him with a poisoned witch's potion."

"What?" I retorted with a snigger. "I never knew my dad. He left us before I was born…" I trailed off. I didn't really want to talk about it with Thomas. Mum never talked about my dad – not ever. With each passing year came a stronger desire to find out more. I should've been more understanding, I suppose. Mum had been through a lot, losing her brother and her parents in one go – in a car accident. I think my dad abandoned her soon after that. Poor Mum but even more, *poor me*. I needed to know more. It was so irritating. I didn't even know what he looked like. Mum had kept no photos of my dad and only a small box of old photos of my grandparents. The only ones left of my late Uncle Win were those of him as a child, looking like any other spotty teenage boy. I did my best to wear Mum down with my frequent outbursts of feeling disconnected.

"I don't even look like you," I used to say. *"I could be anyone from anywhere."*

I thought my friends were so lucky to have dads who grounded them or grandparents who smelled of old socks and farted in public.

As we walked past the old church graveyard of Tribourne Village, there was an abundance of blackberries. I removed the berries one by one, being careful not to touch the thorny brambles, and passed one to Thomas to taste.

"But it hasn't been washed," he said, looking at the juicy berry balanced on my palm.

4

"It doesn't need to be. No one's touched it. It couldn't be cleaner. Try it."

He took the berry and reluctantly popped it into his mouth.

"You need to chew it, Thomas." As I watched him chew, a bit of the juice squirted from his mouth, covering his lips like gothic, black lipstick.

"It's good…really sweet." He nodded.

I encouraged him to pick some, putting them in the box but keeping hold of a few to eat.

"What are these ones down here? Blueberries?"

"No!" I yelled, smacking some shiny, black berries from his grip.

"That's deadly nightshade…the Devil's cherries. The roots are the most poisonous part but the berries have been known to kill children."

Thomas wiped his hands uneasily on his trousers and withdrew from further picking, but I continued conscientiously until the Tupperware box was overflowing. Before reaching home, I collected some wild rosemary from behind the cemetery to put with our vegetable lasagne, which Mum had left in the oven. As I unlocked the front door, a heavenly waft of herby deliciousness greeted our nostrils. Lionel, our highly strung, golden-haired terrier barked, then let out a pathetic grunt before running off to the kitchen to await his dinner. We threw our school bags down in the hallway then followed him.

"It's too early, boy," I said with a giggle, stroking his little head. "Soon…"

"My mum can't get here for a while. I think there's roadworks or something," said Thomas meekly as he looked down at his phone. "I'm sorry. If it's too late, I can just wait outside."

"Don't be daft, Thomas. You can eat with me. It'll be nice to have some male company for a change."

Thomas blushed, making me cringe. I hadn't meant boyfriend male company…just friend male company.

I'm not sure Thomas was that keen when I told him it was vegetarian but he was always munching on something or other at school so I suspected he'd eat whatever I gave him as his stomach would soon get the better of him. Mum was an exceptional cook and could make an amazing meal out of anything.

We broke into some freshly baked bread which was still a bit warm. We didn't use a knife but just tore at the loaf, releasing a cascade of crusty crumbs and a delicious aroma that would linger all night. The smell of Mum's bread always reminded me of everything that was good and safe. It seemed to give Thomas the confidence to try the lasagne.

"I've never eaten anything vegetarian before," he mumbled with a mouthful. "It's really good…really, I mean it."

"Don't sound so surprised." I laughed.

He was now piling on a second helping, chatting away happily and enjoying some animal friendship as Lionel had sat down by his feet, staring at the appealing plate of lasagne, in an effort to capture any dropped food from my guest. We were interrupted by Thomas's phone ringing.

"It's my mum," said Thomas, scoffing down as much of the remaining lasagne as he could before getting tomatoey goo all over his screen as he answered it.

I could just about make out Mrs Marks apologising for being late, then she gave an explanation which I couldn't quite hear. She sounded quite hysterical.

"Are you sure?" said Thomas, still managing to have one more forkful of food. "But it can't be…it can't be." There was a small delay. "Cool! Does this mean I never have to go back to school?"

"What can't be?" I asked, watching Thomas disconnect from his mum. "Why don't you have to go back to school?"

"There's been a fire – an explosion or something…at Saint Timothy's. Apparently the roads are blocked by police cars and fire engines and stuff. My mum's stuck in all the traffic. That's why she's late."

I grabbed my phone off the table and called my mum. She didn't pick up. I texted. I waited. No reply.

"Hey – what are you doing?" asked Thomas, waving his fork at me.

"My mum. She's in the building. I must go and help her," I said, throwing my fleece over my school uniform, then feverishly lacing up my trainers, which was proving difficult as my hands were shaking so much.

"But you'll never get through."

"I'll take my bike round the back, through the cemetery."

"But…it's so creepy this time of day. It's when the light fades and the shadows appear. Besides…you're not honestly planning to go into a burning building, are you? Do you know how dangerous that would be, Ellery?"

"But my mum's in there, Thomas. You coming or not?"

Thomas's face was a picture of horror as he stood there in disbelief, his mouth wide open, revealing bits of unchewed lasagne…but then he smiled, took one last gulp of food, put on his Saint Timothy's blazer and said, "Yep…I'm coming."

"Here…you can borrow Mum's helmet. It's bigger than mine."

Thomas's large head was more than snug as he wrestled with the buckle on Mum's helmet, dark curls escaping from all directions like a cluster of eels. He followed me into the shed round the back of the garden.

"What do you call that?" he snapped.

"It's called a tandem."

"I know what it's called…but how am I supposed to ride that?"

"We're meant to ride it together. Then we can't get separated. C'mon, it's easy…so long as we *both* pedal, of course. I won't be able to pedal for you as well as me."

Thomas was suddenly less enthusiastic but he had no choice and got on the back of the tandem, causing the front to spring up in protest. Thomas ended up on his back, the bike pointing skywards. I removed the handlebars still attached to his hands, brought it to an upright position, then steadied myself on the front, allowing Thomas to remount on the back. Cycling through the cemetery was far less creepy than expected as the roaring blaze from Saint Timothy's seemed to illuminate our path. The thought of Mum, still being inside the school building, sent a fresh wave of panic with resultant jelly legs, making it much more difficult to keep going through the smoke-filled air. Thomas had run out of steam and given up. I couldn't cycle alone carrying my friend's heavy body on the back. I lost my footing and my balance as the bike toppled heavily sideways onto the

8

ground, which was now covered in a layer of grey ash, and I found myself upside down with legs akimbo.

"You okay?" I asked, sliding free from beneath the handlebars and rising quickly to a more dignified position.

"Yep."

We left the bike behind a small bush and continued the rest of the short journey on foot. The smoke was rising vigorously over the school like a sorcerer's cloak engulfing an illusion. Only this was no illusion; I felt my throat burning from the fumes.

"We need to stay hidden," shouted Thomas over the noise of the sirens, "otherwise we'll be sent away."

I nodded.

We walked through the staff car park to face the shock of seeing the library, or more accurately, no library – still smoking with flickering embers glowing eerily in an empty, burned-out shell. Most of the ceiling was hanging down precariously, bits of plasterboard torn apart, exposing electric wiring like human blood vessels. Remnants of book bindings and the odd framework of a chair were all that remained, charred and blackened from the ferocious lick of the flames. I covered my mouth with my hand, which was shaking so badly against my cheeks, it was causing my teeth to chatter. I began hyperventilating, unintentionally inhaling smoke which felt as if I'd placed a burning log into my chest.

"Don't worry," said Thomas. "They never hold the staff meetings in the library. It would've been in the main staffroom. Your mum'll be fine."

I smiled a pathetic smile, a wave of guilt washing over me as my immediate concern was not for my mum but for all the books – all the wonderful stories I'd read and all the ones I'd wanted to read from this library, now lost…all gone forever. My stomach knotted into a painful spasm, making me breathless. The heavy grey smoke blurred before my eyes and I swallowed hard and blinked to focus and prevent hysteria from setting in. If Mum was still in the building, then I'd need to keep calm. Mind you, if Mum was okay then she'd be out of a job as she was the school librarian.

"The only way we can get to the staffroom is through the sixth-form common room," said Thomas.

We headed off, trying to avoid falling debris. We must've been nuts, but the adrenaline seemed to give us a false sense of invincibility. As we entered the common room, the whole area behind us was suddenly engulfed by a set of fiery jaws. The only way out would be through the common room window ahead.

"We can't stay here, Ellery. We'll never make it."

He was right, of course, and I knew we'd have to surrender to safety but something caught my eye…on the floor on the other side of the room. It was a hand, a hand that was clenching and unclenching weakly. It must have belonged to somebody…barely alive.

"It's too dangerous, Ellery."

"We can't just leave them here to die. We must at least try."

I raised my fleece to cover my mouth and nose and Thomas did the same with his Saint Timothy's scarf. We managed to reach the body which was attached to a sixth-form boy, possibly Saint Timothy's head boy for all I knew. A large heavy antique bookcase full of student manuals on further education and *after sixth form* stuff were still contained within the shelves which rested on the poor boy's chest.

"Can't move," he rasped.

"If we get the books out then we might be able to shift the bookcase enough to slide you out," I suggested.

Thomas nodded and we got to work flinging large volumes away from the shelves as quickly as we could while the temperature around us was rising uncomfortably.

"If I try lifting it, then you can pull him free," said Thomas, grabbing a jutting piece of the bookcase.

"Okay."

Thomas was considerably larger than I was so it seemed appropriate that he'd have more strength to lift the bookcase enough for me to free the injured boy.

"Get ready," he said, taking a deep breath as if that would give him added strength.

I grabbed under the arms of the boy, ready for a speedy slide backwards. As I tightened my grip, he clutched at my forearms then gasped loudly, "Stop!"

"What's wrong? You in pain?"

He didn't answer, he just whimpered pathetically. His face twisted into a grimace every time he tried to move.

"I'm so sorry…erm…what's your name?"

"Aiken…my name is Aiken."

"I'm so sorry, Aiken," I began. "We're going to get you out of here, Aiken…I promise. And…you're going to be just fine." I tried to imagine myself as my mum. What would she have said? "You need to be strong…I know you can do it." This was far more difficult than I thought. This boy was practically an adult – he had chin stubble and proper sideburns. He wasn't going to listen to some Year 8 ranting on like a patronising nuisance. "It might hurt for a moment but we're so close now. You're doing really well. Just hang in there."

"Your spell is good. Thank you. Do you know any more spells to help with the pain?"

I looked up at Thomas, whose concentration seemed to be broken by the boy's odd comment.

"What did he say?"

"Dunno," I muttered. "I think he's gone a bit loopy from his injuries. He wants me to do a spell or something."

"He doesn't need a spell – he needs a bloody miracle, Ellery. We're all going to die, it's too heavy," gasped Thomas, looking down at the distressed teenager, drifting in and out of consciousness.

"You!" bellowed a deep and frightening voice from the window.

I froze on the spot as I saw the large, muscular figure to whom the voice belonged. His dark angular face and short, slightly greying, wiry hair accentuated his strong build, the build of someone who knew how to fight, someone unlikely to take sass from anyone. I swallowed with difficulty, my throat so sore. "We need to help him, sir…"

*"You…*sticky boy…"

Thomas, who still had remnants of lasagne round his mouth, pointed at himself in question.

"Yes. Help your girlfriend," he ordered, which turned Thomas's face an embarrassing crimson. The man then climbed nimbly through the window to lift the bookcase from the boy's crumpled chest as if it weighed less than a piece of paper.

We slid him away quickly before the man dropped the heavy bookcase with a thumping crash.

"Who sent you?" he shouted.

"No one," I replied.

"Not you...*you!*" screamed the man, glaring at Aiken, then raising him up roughly by the neck and almost throttling him before pinning him against the blackened wall.

This man frightened me intensely but I couldn't stand there while he killed the defenceless sixth-former. I grabbed his arm to pull his grip from the injured boy's neck. As I did so, he took my arm and twisted it behind my back in a lock. Now he had Aiken in one hand and me in the other.

"This boy has just set your school on fire!" he screamed at me.

I stopped at his shocking statement and he released his grip on me but tightened his grip on Aiken.

"Was it Saxon Nash? Did he make you do this?"

The boy said nothing.

"Answer me, boy! Is this his new plan? To destroy Dweller schools and books? To kill the teachers? To hit vulnerable schoolchildren? Answer me, boy. Answer me!" He was shaking Aiken, who despite being covered in soot, was as white as a sheet, tears running furiously down his cheeks, leaving white streaks either side.

"You can't kill me. I'm still a teenager. It's not our way... and you know it. You can't hurt a youngling...you can't."

Youngling? I was starting to wonder if I'd stumbled onto a *Star Wars* film-set. Who would use the word 'youngling', apart from Obi-Wan Kenobi? Squinting through the smoke, I tried to scrutinise this large, intimidating man more closely, slightly disappointed by not spotting a lightsabre hanging off his trouser belt.

The injured boy had become red in the face.

"Youngling? *Youngling?*" snapped the man. "You've got more facial hair than I have!"

"I seriously doubt that," I whispered to Thomas, watching the boy slump to the floor as the large man sent a vicious slap in his direction. He then hoisted the unconscious teenager over his shoulder and ushered us to the window.

"My mum…" I choked, as I clambered through.

"Who do you think sent me to find you? She's fine, by the way…very lucky…very lucky indeed. She'd left the staffroom to get some more mugs from the canteen when the explosion hit. Your headmaster, on the other hand, wasn't so lucky. He might not make it. Such an unnecessary waste," he shouted over the noise of fire-engine sirens, looking pensively ahead as he led us away from the building.

"My mother *knows* you?"

The man ignored me. "What you did was madness – you know that, don't you? What were you thinking, strolling into a burning building like that? And *you*…sticky boy…you went along with her."

"Thomaaaaas! Thomas Marks! How dare you go off like that. I've been worried sick."

"You must be the boy's…erm…older sister? I'm Hendrick Myerscough." He extended his arm for a handshake.

Thomas and I both groaned at Hendrick Myerscough's lame line.

"Prunella Marks." She giggled, holding out her hand to shake Myerscough's. "Thomas's *mother* actually."

Thomas's mum had a round freckled face framed with a mane of curly, dark hair which was peppered with grey. Her waistline was quite large, causing her to topple as she struggled to keep her balance over her high heels, but she was still tiny next to Myerscough. I reckon he was the biggest person I'd ever met.

"Your son has behaved recklessly and deserves your reprimand. However, as his friend could not be dissuaded from searching for her mother at the school, young Thomas here took it upon himself to look after Ellery in her quest. This was quite possibly the bravest thing he's ever undertaken in his young life, and it must not go unnoticed that he managed to save the life of a fellow pupil. He knew the danger involved and yet he still took the risk. I think he deserves to be commended. Bloody foolhardy, if you ask me…but bloody brave all the same."

Mrs Marks stood silent, looking at her son like a complete stranger. "Are you sure it was Thomas?"

"You need to give the boy some credit, Madam. Now if you'll excuse me…I need to get this young lady back to her mother." He took my arm and began marching me in the direction of the fire crew and ambulances, where I saw Mum, sooty-faced and waving with a very relieved smile.

"Mr Myerscough?" I asked.

"What?"

"Why would Aiken want to burn the school down?"

"This is neither the time nor the place for explanations. I'll take you and your mum home. We'll talk there."

"Who's Saxon Nash?"

Myerscough looked surprised that I didn't know but made no attempt to answer my question and I certainly wasn't going to challenge his decision. He frightened the life out of me.

2

THE TRUTH

"Lionel…we're back, boy," said Mum as she turned on the light in the hall. Lionel was not amused at having been abandoned for most of the evening and left in the dark into the bargain. He chose to ignore both me and Mum. He didn't, however, ignore Myerscough and ran straight over to greet him.

"Traitor," said Mum, with a giggle. "Here." She threw him a treat from her pocket, causing him to instantly switch allegiance. We took off our smoky-smelling coats and walked into the messy kitchen.

"Sorry," I said. "We left in a bit of a hurry."

"You demolished the lasagne, I see," said Mum. "Not to worry. I'm not hungry anyway. All I can taste is smoke." She poured two glasses of red wine, one for herself and the other for Myerscough.

"One for the road, Hendrick?"

"But—" I protested, putting my hands on my hips. "But you said you'd talk once we were home. You said you'd explain…" I was about to launch into a hissy fit when the doorbell interrupted me. I stormed out of the room into the hall to open the front door onto the soot-covered fleshy face of Thomas Marks.

"I brought your tandem back," he said. "We left it, remember?"

"Yeh, thanks…I'd forgotten."

He paused for a moment before awkwardly blurting out something inaudible.

"What was that?"

"Do you want to hang out some time…? If you've nothing better to do, that is. Only if you want. Nah…course not. Silly idea really. Silly. Sorry."

"Sure, I'd love to."

His face lit up.

As he left I shouted after him, "Thank you…for coming with me tonight."

"That's what friends are for, right?" He smiled. "We *are* friends, aren't we?"

"The best."

He smiled again, more broadly than before and waved as he climbed into his mum's car.

As I shut the front door, I could hear raised voices.

"You haven't told her much, have you N?"

"What do you mean? And the name is Nuala."

"You know what I mean. She doesn't know *anything*…"

"She doesn't need to either…not yet anyway."

"She needs to know the truth, *Nuala*. The truth."

18

"I'm not losing her, Hendrick. I need to protect her. If she's kept away, she'll be safe."

"If she's kept in the dark, she will be anything but safe. Nash will find her…and you…"

I could hear my mum sobbing.

"Nuala…she's…"

"I'm what? Tell me… What am I?" I had no idea what was going on and pursed my lips in anger.

Myerscough took a large swig of his red wine before clearing his throat. My mother was looking anxiously across at him.

"She needs to know the truth, Nuala. At least something…"

Mum closed her eyes in resignation while Myerscough gestured with a flick of his head for me to take a seat. His whole persona carried such power and authority. He wasn't threatening me and yet I knew I must do as he commanded. I sat down ready to listen. I was going to do my best not to interrupt. My heart was banging hard against my chest and an odd sensation passed through me, sending a weakening chill down my spine.

"I suggest you let go of that breath, young Ellery, or you might die before you find out the information you so desperately seek."

I breathed out, which seemed to calm me slightly.

"I…am a Magaecian."

"*Right*…of course you are," I responded, having quickly come to the assumption that he must be yet another loony that Mum was friends with. "Shouldn't you have a wand or something?"

said Mageeeeyshun, not magician, cloth ears," he shouted as he swung an old newspaper left on the kitchen table, walloping me on the top of the head with it.

"Is there a difference? I mean, you do spells, right? Aiken…back in the fire…he asked me to chant a spell."

Myerscough grunted again. "Aiken Thorne, poor boy… just an unfortunate pawn causing collateral damage. A spell or spells is just a group of *spellings* that make up words and sentences. So Aiken wanted you to utter a *spell*…a sentence or two that would calm him and make him feel better."

"Oh, I see." I sighed, quite disappointed that there wasn't any *actual* magic involved.

"Spells, or words, if you like, can be very powerful. They can injure so much more than any weapon. For example, a 'word' can be turned into a sharp instrument just by putting an 's' in front of it; or you may become evil if you live backwards."

"What?" I hissed. This man was talking rubbish.

"The word, LIVE – spell it backwards – EVIL."

"I know," I retorted, annoyed that I hadn't figured out his palindrome more quickly. "Well, what about *sticks and stones may break my bones but names will never hurt me?*" I asked, leaning across the table.

"What about it?" he snapped, causing me to retract quickly. "Sticks and stones may hurt you but those wounds will heal. Spells, however, may cause devastating and long-lasting injury. Our feelings are vital to our well-being so never underestimate the power of spells. Once they have been pronounced, they cannot be retracted…so take heed."

"Sticks and stones may break your bones but words can

break your heart," added Mum. "I think that's from i
isn't it?"

"One wrong word can change the meaning of a whole
conversation," continued Myerscough, ignoring Mum's
passing comment. "Perhaps the very balance between war
and peace."

It was an odd way to see words and yet, his explanation
made perfect sense.

"Your father is a Magaecian, Ellery, and you have a right
to know the Magaecian way."

"My dad's a Magaecian? Why didn't you tell me this,
Mum? Why didn't you tell me?" I could feel myself going
red in the face but decided to withdraw when I saw how
distressed Mum was looking. She could hardly catch her
breath as she clutched at her throat. My emotions were all
over the place; upset, confused, angry…and for what? I still
had no idea what a Magaecian even was.

"You see, to explain properly, I need to tell you about a
man called Darwin Burgess who was head of the Magaecian
Circle," began Myerscough.

"The Magaecian Circle?"

"Yes. The Circle was made up of thirteen members. The
head, Darwin Burgess, plus twelve others." Myerscough's
eyes seemed to be penetrating my own as I hung on his every
word. I had so many questions but I let him continue.

"The Magaecian Circle was a select group. Just before
Darwin was killed, it consisted of me, Bentley Davenport…
still in hiding, so they say; Faye Holton, who also hasn't
been seen for over a decade; Aldora Huckabee, one of our
finest, a handsome woman…a good egg," said Myerscough,

clearing his throat before continuing. "Saxon Nash, of course, and the rest of the Circle was made up mainly of Nash's hideous followers like Gibson Hastings…nasty piece of work…Kimberley and Knox Nibley-Soames, Preston Hayes, Rohesia and Wade Tattersall, unscrupulous lot, all of them…and then…poor Corliss. Corliss Winterbourne, who never came to terms with what happened to her…"

"What happened to her?"

"Some things are best left unsaid," replied Myerscough curtly.

"Does the Circle still exist?" I asked, rapidly changing the subject from the obviously *not to be mentioned* Corliss Winterbourne.

"Hardly," answered Myerscough. "Well…a new Magaecian Circle exists but with all Nash's followers. None of the other members are on it. We used to work beside non-Magaecians. We call them Magaedwells. We worked alongside prime ministers, presidents, kings and queens from all over the world. You with me so far?"

"What are Magaedwells?"

"Magaedwells or Dwellers are people that *dwell* on Magae but don't follow the Magaecian way." His angular chin seemed to have an agenda all of its own and suddenly posed a great threat to me. It was like a skin-covered weapon, a *chin-buster* that could be removed from his face at any moment to clobber me to death, if I didn't understand.

"Magaecians are from Magae," he barked.

"Magey?" I repeated, fearful of another reprimanding outburst.

"Magae. *Ma* from the colloquial word meaning *mother*

and...*ge* is from the Greek word meaning Earth...a.
as Gaea, of course, by the Ancient Greeks. Mother Ea.
Mother Nature...*your planet*. We respect Magae as a living
entity that allows us to inhabit her."

"I don't really understand."

Mum took my hand, then looked at Myerscough.

"Magaecians," he started, "believe that Earth is not
ours...we're simply allowed to inhabit her and share its
amenities with other living things. Magae adapts to her needs
of survival. When man first inhabited Magae, we were all
Magaecians. We were all able to use our senses and instincts
to survive. That meant sensing when a storm was brewing,
seeing a moving creature that might well eat us, finding a safe
shelter, gathering food. We lived together with other animals
and plants alike, respecting each other's right for survival. If
something threatened Magae, she would manage to restore
balance, whether that be changing the planet's temperature
or restoring the atmosphere's gases. It just meant that she
could regulate an optimum living condition which in turn
would make it safe to continue living on her without causing
her harm."

I was nodding.

Myerscough continued. "Like I said...everyone on Earth
started life as a Magaecian, respecting our planet, but as the
world moved on, so most forgot their Magaecian roots and
opted out of the Magaecian way."

"So why haven't I ever heard of Magaecians?"

"Because people think they're bad – sorcerers and
black-magic makers," answered Mum. "They're actually
just people from Magae...but stories become distorted over

time. Most feel safer keeping a low profile in such troubled times…" Mum stopped herself as tears welled up in her eyes, prompting Myerscough to put his large hand on her shoulder in comfort, although I suspect it felt more like a crippling, bone-crunching grip.

"Poor Darwin worked tirelessly on a very important mission…the most important, in fact. The human race is causing such damage to Magae that she will soon be unable to recover," added Myerscough.

"So it's all about saving the planet," I said, feeling quite proud of myself for reaching the answer in spite of the cryptic clues these two adults were throwing at me.

"No!" roared Myerscough in disappointment. "No…the planet will look after itself. Magae can always find a way to recover. She always has and always will."

"I don't understand."

"What would you do if something was making you ill, Ellery?"

"I don't know. Get Mum to make up a herbal remedy or take me to the doctor for an antibiotic?"

"Why? What would that do?"

"Get rid of it, I suppose." As I answered, Myerscough raised his eyebrows and leaned his head forward in a gesture for me to continue with an answer…the right answer which I definitely didn't have.

"And?"

"And…" I had no idea of the answer expected of me. I only knew that I must reach it or risk Myerscough's wrath if I didn't. Myerscough's words had filled my head, going round and round in an endless circle of nothing…until a thought did enter and I suddenly saw a clearer picture. "Wait…"

"Yes…yes?"

"You're saying that if we continue to damage Magae…"

"Yes…go on…"

"If we continue to damage Magae…then she'll find a way to get rid of…*us*? So it's not the planet that needs to be saved, is it? It's…us. She needs to rid herself of us to stay alive, doesn't she?"

Myerscough was looking at me with raised eyebrows again. "I guess you're not as stupid as you look after all."

I thought it best not to comment although it was quite an effort to hold my tongue.

"Darwin Burgess was trying to get this point across. We're an endangered species. If we don't respect Magae, she will make her planet uninhabitable for us. We need to work together, Magaecians and Dwellers alike. We need to educate, re-educate in fact, so that we have a chance of remaining on the planet."

"But how?"

"I could go on and on…but I think that should be left to a more appropriate time. There's so much that needs addressing. Most schools don't tell kids much in case it *worries* them. It's ridiculous…and it *should* worry them. It's an emergency that needs confronting now. Darwin had a number of policies to put in place but Nash was in constant opposition. He thought that if only Magaecians – and not Dwellers – lived on Magae, then the problem would no longer exist. He thought the solution was…" Myerscough stopped mid-sentence and looked down at the kitchen floor, exhaling loudly.

"Was what? What was the solution?"

"The solution was...simple. Rid the planet of Dwellers, of course."

"What do you mean?"

Myerscough raised his eyebrows once more as if the answer should be obvious.

"You don't mean...?"

Myerscough nodded.

"Kill them all?"

Myerscough nodded again. "It goes against all Magaecian law, of course. We don't harm other living beings. It is not the Magaecian way."

I found that difficult to believe, coming from someone who walloped a defenceless teenager unconscious less than an hour ago.

"We respect all living things from the tiniest bug to the largest wildebeest. We only kill if it's absolutely necessary... life or death...which is what Nash believes it to be. We are not like him. He gives us a bad name."

"So would he kill a fellow Magaecian?"

"If he thought there was no other choice. You know? A life-threatening situation to the survival of the Magaecian people. It is not a path Magaecians usually follow...but Nash is no usual Magaecian."

"So, was he responsible for Darwin Burgess's death?"

Mum got up, tearing off some kitchen roll, using it to stifle her sobs.

"Nash is a very powerful man with many fans. Those who oppose him risk his vengeful retaliation."

"How could any right-minded person agree to this

way of thinking? It's cold-blooded murder," sobbed Mum, heading into the hallway.

"Mr Myerscough…surely Saxon Nash risked losing his followers by murdering another Magaecian…and not just any Magaecian but the head of the Magaecian Circle. So why did he kill Darwin Burgess?"

"Because Darwin Burgess was not a Magaecian."

"What?"

"He was born a Dweller but learned the Magaecian way. Being brought up as a Dweller made him a better Magaecian, some say. He understood the mind of a Dweller and knew how he could set about changing it. He had great insight and was accepted by many as a great Magaecian, but Nash insisted that he wasn't a *true* Magaecian and never would be. He even thought that mixed marriages were wrong and should be discouraged in order to save the Magaecian race. Huh! F–"

Mum shook her head from the doorway and stared wide-eyed at him, glancing fleetingly in my direction as he was about to swear in front of me.

"Fff…limflam, piffle and…nonsense!"

I was shocked. Not by his use of ridiculous, less than colourful swear words, but by all this information which was too much for me to process.

"It's madness. Being a Magaecian is a way of life. It's not a religion and it doesn't make you different as a species. You don't have three hands or yellow eyes. You're still just a human. You choose to respect your planet and see the world in a different way. Nothing more…nothing less."

"What are we going to do?" asked Mum, wiping away

her tears.

"Oh, Nuala, Ellery needs an E.S.S. She's the age now. You know they start in the year they turn a decade and three."

"What's that? I'm not seeing some shrink or taking drugs that I don't need," I yelled.

"It's a school." Myerscough laughed. "An Earth Science School…E.S.S."

I stopped puffing and let out a sigh, feeling like a bit of a twit. "What's an Earth Science School?"

"It's a school for Magaecians."

"Where is it?" I asked.

"It's nowhere in particular. It's a travelling school," replied Myerscough with a smile. "It moves through the year all round the countryside…over oceans in the older years. It allows you to learn and appreciate different terrains… re-wild yourself. We practise the Quinton Earth Science Teachings…your personal QUEST using the FIVE elements to be:

F lexible and

I mprovise,

V anquish and

E mpathise while respecting Earth and its Air, Fire, Water and Space."

"Cool! I'm in," I said enthusiastically despite not having a clue what he was on about.

"Good," replied the large man with a nod.

"It's not safe," interrupted Mum.

"I'm going. You can't stop me." I had to admit, it sounded a hundred times better than Saint Timothy's and that was now a pile of rubble anyway.

"You need to let go, Nuala. Besides…she'll be a lot safer with me than with you."

Mum gave no reply as her teeth appeared to lock together.

"There is one condition though…" I added.

"I beg your pardon?" snapped Myerscough.

"I have one condition if you want me to join your Earth School."

"It's called The Quinton Earth Science School, named after Scott Quinton, a Magaecian legend…and I'm not open to conditions."

"I'm not coming then."

"She's just like her father," said Mum, laughing.

"She's nothing like her father," Myerscough snapped again.

"I want my friends to come. They have no school now that Saint Timothy's has gone…and it's our fault as Magaecians that it has."

"But an E.S.S. is only for Magaecian children, Ellery," replied Myerscough with a heavy sigh.

"Mr Myerscough, what's the point of teaching Magaecians how to respect their planet when they already know? It's the non-Magaecians…the Dwellers that need to be taught…from Magaecians…at Magaecian schools. We need to teach *them*. All of them."

Myerscough looked across to my mum with narrowed eyes. "I can see your daughter's going to be nothing but trouble."

"I do hope so," said Mum with a smile.

"Okay. Meet me at the old abandoned Tribourne Hotel, 22nd September. Our term starts here this year, our chosen meeting point before setting off on our school travels. It's when autumn officially begins…and we finish 21st December when autumn ends. So you have three days to get your daughter sorted. I'll speak to the governors at Saint Timothy's but I doubt we'll have many takers. They tend not to like our kind."

3

INTRODUCTIONS AND ALTERCATIONS

Mum dropped me at the old Tribourne Hotel with a number of bags and belongings. It was a weary-looking building that needed attention. Large decaying double doors barely holding on by their rusty hinges were an unwelcoming reminder of its melancholy abandonment. I anticipated a long and drawn-out goodbye from Mum but she seemed preoccupied, on edge and jumpy. She kept looking around and behind her in anxious anticipation. I knew she was worried about me going off, but I actually felt a little disappointed at not getting the cringeworthy heartfelt farewell I'd been dreading. It was weird.

"Say your goodbyes in here," said Myerscough, shepherding us into a little side room. "She'll be fine, Nuala. I'll be watching her. You have my word."

Mum was crying now, which was kind of embarrassing but she managed to compose herself enough to give me a huge hug. "Be careful, Ellery. You have a reckless courage that seriously worries me, darling. Be patient with your new teachers and friends and be prepared to accommodate and adapt. But most importantly...be you. I love you, sweetheart."

"I love you too, Mum. I'll be fine. Tough and resilient... that's me."

Mum touched my face and smiled. She hugged Myerscough which was pretty brave, then she left. I probably should've been more emotional but instead I was excited, mixed in with quite a bit of nerves, my insides like a swirling vortex. Myerscough led me out onto a hallway and then into a very large and grand room. Possibly a ballroom in its day but quite clearly an assembly hall today. The noise hit me like a slap in the face as soon as he opened the door. The room was packed with pupils all chatting and laughing.

"Ellery!"

I turned to see Letty walking towards me.

"Letty...I'm so pleased you're here. Is Billy here?"

Letty looked back at me in disappointment as she shook her head. "His parents said it was no place for their son and that he should have nothing more to do with me if I went."

"Oh...I see. I'm sorry, I really am."

"Hi," blurted out a tall, skinny boy, bending down to poke his face between us. "I'm Fenwick Barclay, I'm in the sixth form. This is my younger brother, Kemp. He's new today too."

Kemp was an average-sized boy with a thin, pale face. His haunting grey eyes reflected a look of embarrassment as his older brother was obviously enjoying his position of power in the sixth form.

"Excuse me for a moment, I'm going to talk to that stocky boy over there. He looks a bit lost, doesn't he?"

"That's Thomas. We know him. Thomas!" I shouted, but he didn't hear me. "Thomas Marks!"

He looked round in bewilderment then a beaming smile seemed to fill the whole room. He waved as he headed towards us.

"Mum didn't want me to come. She said she'd miss me too much but Dad thought it a good idea…probably so that he wouldn't have to worry about forgetting to pick me up when it's his turn."

"I'm sure that's not the case, Thomas."

"Mind you…Mum only let me come when she heard you'd be here. She said you were a good influence and brought out the best in me."

"Really? I think *you* bring out the best in you, Thomas… not me."

"What's *she* doing here?" asked Letty, spotting Irene Sturrage heading in our direction. Irene Sturrage, the goody two shoes who had every teacher wrapped around her little finger. She was about as sweet as a spoonful of tahini! However, as she got closer, it wasn't Irene at all but a girl that looked uncannily like her.

"Phew!" said Letty. "Let's hope her personality isn't similar."

"Why?" asked Kemp, who had been listening to us chatter.

"You'd understand if you knew her," answered Letty, giving him a flirtatious smile. It didn't seem to take her long to get over Billy.

"Silence, please!" screamed a man from the back of the hall. "Your headmistress wishes to address you."

A stocky woman with a silver bun came to the front of the room. She was dressed in a grey skirt and cream blouse that was so full of frills she appeared to have no neck or chin, all swallowed up in chiffon. She casually put on some rimless spectacles which heightened her bright blue eyes against her soft pink, marshmallow-like skin.

"Welcome back, everyone. For those of you who are new today…Year 8," she added, pulling her glasses halfway down her nose, then looking over them in our direction. "I am Mrs Huckabee, headmistress of The Quinton Earth Science School."

"Huckabee? That can't be a real name, can it?" whispered Letty.

I shrugged.

"After an unfortunate fire at Saint Timothy's, we find ourselves in the charge of some temporary students who wish to learn more about their Earth."

There was a drone of voices whispering their disapproval.

"Bloody pliskies shouldn't be here," said a dark-haired, dark-eyed boy to my right.

"What's a plisky?" I asked.

"Never mind," replied Kemp. "Just ignore him. That's Orford Nibley-Soames. His parents are fierce followers of Saxon Nash. They're all raving nutcases, if you ask me."

As I scanned the hall, I recognised no one from Saint Timothy's apart from Letty and Thomas. Surely Myerscough had convinced more pupils than that? I was disappointed.

"It is our Magaecian duty to help them and guide them and befriend them through this difficult time…" continued Mrs Huckabee. "As we travel through our studies, your friendships will grow and many lifelong bonds will be formulated. But you must remember, younglings, that these are troubled times in which we live and there will be very real dangers lurking on your travels, so be mindful. Be prepared to listen and obey your tutors no matter what. They have only your best interests at heart. Be positive, be adventurous, be captivated…but be flexible and wise and most of all…be honest…then you can't fail to enjoy your time together. So many old students return to tell me that their days with our school were the best days of their lives." She stopped for a quick swig of water, cleared her throat, then continued.

"We operate a *rainbow* system here. This means that all students start on neutral, which is green. If you do well here and thrive, then your colour will change from green to blue; better than blue is indigo, then best of all is violet. Finishing term above green is a real achievement and something you should all strive to attain. However, if you do not do well… not just in studies but in your behaviour, then you will be given a yellow. Continued misconduct will lead to orange and then finally…red. I don't want to see anyone on red."

"It's like getting a football penalty." Thomas laughed.

I smiled. I wondered how bad you had to be to get a red and whether it meant you'd be sent off, or in this case, sent home or expelled.

"Your tutors will select a pupil to come to my provisional office after assembly to pick up a supply of each year's timetable. The rest of you may return with your tutor to your temporary classrooms for information on lessons, travelling and necessary equipment."

I felt a heavy grip on my shoulder, which made me jump.

"You can pick up the timetables, please," said Myerscough.

"Sure. Where do I go, sir?"

"Just follow the others. Someone will redirect you back to me afterwards."

Myerscough left with my classmates and I followed the other selected *timetable monitors* to the headmistress. As we approached, Mrs Huckabee was having an argument with some tall, skinny-looking man. His face was frighteningly gaunt, heightened by dark, dark eyebrows and steely grey hair.

"That's Gibson Hastings," said a freckle-faced girl fiddling with her ponytail. She grabbed her pile of Year 11 timetables, then whispered, "He's on the Magaecian Circle, you know."

"How can you entertain these pliskies?"

"Mr Hastings, that's hardly the language we deem appropriate at a school. Please refrain from using such a derogatory term with younglings present."

"I apologise. You're right, but these...these Dweller children," he continued, turning up his nose. "They have no right to be here. Their kind have ruined the planet we love. They have no respect for Magae...none. They're an insult to all of us." The man stopped and looked at me. I'd been unaware of my obvious eavesdropping and felt my face become very hot and I suspect very red.

"*You*, girl." He pointed at me, causing my face to grow hotter still. "Come here."

I didn't dare disobey and walked over to him as ordered.

"What's your name, girl?"

"Ellery, sir. Ellery Brown."

"A good Magaecian name."

"Thank you, sir. I think it's an old English name."

The man smiled. "What's your opinion on these scummy Dwellers invading your school, Ellery? Do you think they deserve a place here even though they are not Magaecian?"

I could see Mrs Huckabee shaking her head in disapproval. The man was deeply unpleasant. No wonder Myerscough called him a nasty piece of work.

"Well?" he added impatiently.

"Well, sir," I began, "I think you're probably right in that Dwellers are not Magaecians…"

Hastings was nodding and smiling.

"But…all Magaecians *dwell* on Magae, don't they, which means, I guess, that all Magaecians are also Dwellers. Maybe we're not so different after all."

"Perhaps we should work on that," added Mrs Huckabee, hastily attempting to halt my awkward conversation with Hastings.

"How dare you compare Magaecians to the scum of the Earth…pliskies that will get us all killed. Obnoxious fools… all of them."

"I think perhaps you mean *ignorant* not obnoxious, which is why we must be more clement and exercise untold intolerance to injustice and prejudice, no matter how egregious they may seem," butted in Mrs Huckabee, looking down her spectacles sternly and passing me a wad of timetables and a signal with her head to get going before I got myself into deeper water. She certainly had great power with her words and managed to silence the loathsome Hastings with minimal effort. Half those words she used I'd never even heard before. I was beginning to see the importance of spells and the power they commanded.

"At least the Dwellers are here only temporarily. As soon as Saint Timothy's is up and running again, they can return to their own school," said Hastings, red-faced and puffing.

"So long as you don't burn it to the ground again," I muttered under my breath as I left the room, without a clue as to where I was meant to be going to get back to Myerscough.

***

"Mother Earth, Ellery! What took you so long?" hollered Myerscough as I handed him the timetables. "Don't give them to *me*! Hand them out."

I passed them round then sat on the floor next to Thomas. The room was surrounded by musical instruments.

"Magaecians like their music," whispered Kemp on noticing my curiosity. "All Magaecian families play something or other, or sing," he added.

Letty had already got out her tiny sketch pad, something she always carried around with her. She began drawing the many instruments. I picked up a timetable and glanced at it quickly. I noticed a double period of *Chocomestry*, but I got no further as Mrs Huckabee stood in the doorway summoning Myerscough to let her speak with "Miss Brown, please". My heart sank. Here it comes, I thought. A yellow card for speaking out to Gibson Hastings. Myerscough summoned me with a flick of his hand.

"Mrs Huckabee…I'm sorry," I said, stepping out into the hallway. "I think I upset your friend. I didn't mean to."

"Miss Brown, let me make this quite clear. He's *not* my friend. I've not come to reprimand you but to commend you on your obvious gift of casting a spell. You're a natural. I'm guessing you must read a lot."

"My mum's a librarian so it's inevitable, I suppose."

"Yes, indeed. My only criticism here, Ellery, is that Gibson Hastings is a very powerful and dangerous man… as are all those that follow Saxon Nash. You must, in certain situations, bite your tongue. May I suggest erring on the side of caution in future. Patience may be a virtue here…do you see? You are your own spell keeper and it is up to you to cast wisely. Our spells may allow us to rise above the beasts but they may also submerge us below the furies if we are not careful. Do you understand?"

"Yes, Miss. I understand."

"Good."

"Mrs Huckabee?"

"Yes, dear?"

"What's a…*plisky*?"

"Ah…yes. Well, it's not really a spell I would choose to use…but if you must know, it means a practical joke. It implies that Dwellers are one big joke to be laughed at."

"I see."

"Just remember, Ellery, there is little humour in power but great power in humour." She smiled then added, "Something to chew on, don't you think?"

I smiled in agreement then headed back to my class, who had formed an orderly queue by the doorway.

"Follow me," said Myerscough. His voice was so abrupt and fierce and still frightened me far too much.

"Where are we going?" I asked, getting in the queue next to a tall, white-blonde Magaecian boy.

"Chocomestry," he whispered.

"What's that?"

"The chemistry of chocolate, of course."

"Cool!"

"I know. It's totally Hawk!"

"Totally what?"

The boy started to laugh. "You don't live around Magaecians much, do you? Totally Hawk! You know… amazing…only *more*!"

"Right. Totally Hawk."

"I'm Nyle Pinkerton."

"Hi, Nyle. I'm Ellery – Ellery Brown."

4

CHOCOMESTRY

Chocomestry took part in the old kitchen, which was enormous and cold. I could see my breath freezing in front of my eyes as I blew on my frozen fingers.

"Come in, come in. Apologies for the chill. I've had to restart the old freezer. It should warm up in a minute or two...especially once you start mixing."

As I looked across at Thomas, he was jumping up and down. I'm not sure I'd ever seen him smile so widely. Mind you, chocolate chemistry...how could he not be excited?

"Now, younglings...for those of you who don't know me, I'm Dr Ramsay, PhD in cocoabutterfication on which I've written several papers...and of course, I write a monthly column in the B.C.M.J., the *British Choco-Medical Journal*."

Letty was doing her best to stifle her giggles but it was quite contagious and I found myself snorting to the dissatisfaction of my new teacher, who looked a bit like a

41

puffin. She was quite pretty but her nose was curvy like a beak.

"Take an overall from the front here, then stand beside a pestle and mortar on the work table please," yelled Dr Ramsay. Her voice echoed round the large room, bouncing off the thick stone walls before hitting the dusty red quarry tiles on the floor. She then proceeded to go through a set of instructions, pointing out the various nutritional and medicinal properties associated with *proper* chocolate. A selection of poorly drawn diagrams, scribbled on a presentation board, had been placed strategically to face the students. The lighting was so dim and gloomy, if you weren't directly facing the board the black letters seemed to dissolve into the shadows.

We crushed our cocoa beans, releasing an instant aroma of chocolate into the atmosphere. I continued to follow the instructions for a fine paste…only mine looked more like lumpy porridge and Thomas had more on his face than in the bowl. We were given the choice of adding coconut sugar or cane sugar, plus a pinch of salt, which made my mixture even more lumpy. I was pleased to see that I wasn't the only one finding it tiring as many of the class had rolled up their sleeves to give their crushing some real elbow grease. Dr Ramsay commended Letty on her smooth, paste-like mixture. She poured melted cocoa butter into each pupil's bowl, followed by a special *tempered* chocolate for a smooth, glossy finish, apparently vital for that satisfying *snap* when broken. We were passed around tablet-shaped moulds with an impression of the school crest, which would no doubt be embossed on the finished chocolate once it had set.

"I'm passing round some chocolate that I made last week," said Dr Ramsay, nodding or tutting as she peered into everyone's chocolatey bowl. "Smell it…it's smoky. The beans are brought over by Mrs Wan from Tawau, where the soil is volcanic."

Thomas was sniffing so hard I thought he might inhale it up his nose.

"Now put it to your ear. Can anybody hear anything?"

"Is it the sea, Miss?" called out Aldwyn Garrick.

"I meant listen to the sound when you break it, dimwit. It should be a crisp snap."

Aldwyn sighed with embarrassment as an audible snigger passed round the room.

"Write your names at the bottom of the moulds and leave them on the work table. They'll be ready this afternoon. A good, healthy snack to give you that boost you might need to take on your term's peregrination, which starts tomorrow."

"The term's what?" whispered Letty.

"Peregrination. It's our school journey…our travel from one place to another," answered Kemp.

"Can we lick the chocolate left over in our bowls, Dr Ramsay?" called out Delia Wu.

"It appears some have already done so," she answered, looking over in our direction as Thomas had managed to give himself a chocolate moustache.

"Once you've tidied up and returned your aprons you may go back to your tutor room for any money etc. to spend at the shops on snacks during break time. Don't carry a load of bags with you…leave them in the tutor room, please. Your teacher will run through a few rules after lunch, served in the grounds here, as you've a small excursion this afternoon. You may purchase any snack items you like but be sensible. No fizzy drinks and no rubbish, please."

While carrying out Dr Ramsay's instructions, I was nudged hard in the back by Orford Nibley-Soames. "She said no *rubbish*. You three better not come then. Besides… your days on this planet are numbered anyway, Plisky."

"All of our days on this planet are numbered, Orford… not just mine."

"'All of our days on this planet are numbered, Orford'," he repeated in a high-pitched sarcastically squeaky voice. "Plisky scum."

"Seriously? Plisky scum? Is that really the best you can do?" I could feel Letty trying to pull me away. "Plisky's not even that bad a word. It means a practical joke. Big deal."

"Because that's what you are, Brown – all of you – a joke."

"At least humour hails from an agile wit…bullying hails from a brainless git!" I barely had time to finish my rant which, for a spur of the moment improv' was pretty good, if I do say so myself…when Nibley-Soames threw an almighty punch that sent me flying. It wasn't his punch that knocked me over but Thomas's body crashing into mine as he had stood in front of me to take the full impact of the strike.

"Stop immediately!" yelled Dr Ramsay, standing between Nibley-Soames, the fallen Thomas nursing a bloody nose, and myself. "How dare you!" she growled sternly. "Get up!" She slammed her hands onto her hips. "Right then – let's have Mr Barclay and…your friend…Miss…"

"Letty, Miss," added Letty.

"Yes...Miss Letty. Please take Mr Marks to see Dr Wilberforce on the second floor. The rest of you may return to your tutor room for your belongings. As for you two..." Dr Ramsay was seriously flustered, her face a shade of purple and her nostrils flaring wildly. "Mr Nibley-Soames...that's a yellow...and it's a yellow for you too, Miss Brown."

I watched a smirk appear on Nibley-Soames's face.

"Violence is unacceptable here. You are treading on very thin ice if you continue down this slippery path."

"Wait until my mother hears about this," mumbled Nibley-Soames. "She's on the school governor's board and she's a member of the Magaecian Circle. She and Dad are very close with Saxon Nash, you know?"

"Yes, I did know and quite frankly I don't care if they're high priest and priestess to Superman!" screamed Dr Ramsay, her voice at least two octaves higher than usual. "I will be watching you – *both* of you from now on, so tread carefully." She snatched her pile of moth-eaten notes, then stormed out.

I ran up to the second floor to meet my friends who, luckily, were exiting Dr Wilberforce's room, so I didn't need to guess which of the many doors to try.

"Thanks, Thomas. I owe you one," I puffed.

"You were egging him on, Ellery," said Kemp. "You were asking for trouble. Nibley-Soames's mum and dad are very close to Nash. They'll have Ramsay fired for that."

I suddenly felt a deep pang of guilt for behaving in my usual *speak before I think* mode. Poor Dr Ramsay. She didn't deserve to be fired on my account.

"Your name will now be in Nibley-Soames's limited vocabulary, which means his mum and dad will be watching you too…and anyone that mixes with you."

"Well done, Ellery." Letty sighed.

"I don't think you understand, Ellery. These are dangerous people," Kemp began sincerely. "We all want to change the world but you can't do it if you get yourself killed before you've had the chance."

"I'm sorry. I didn't know. I mean, I didn't think. Sorry."

"C'mon," said Letty, raising the sombre mood. "Let's go to the shops for snacks. Does anyone need to go back to the tutor room for cash? I've got my money on me."

"I do," I said. "I'll meet you at the shops."

I ran down to the tutor room to hunt for my purse, which I'd left right at the bottom of my rucksack. As I picked up my bag, written in capital letters broadly across it in bright neon yellow marker was the word P L I S K Y. It wasn't just my bag but Letty's and Thomas's too. I was so angry. There were so many thoughts going through my mind…how to have my vengeance on Orford Nibley-Soames. However, I paused as I thought about what Kemp had said. Besides, I had no proof it was definitely Nibley-Soames. I stood in muted contemplation. I wasn't going to act before thinking… not this time. That is, not until I saw the bright yellow writing on the wall…

OUT PLISKY TRASH!

***

I reached the local supermarket breathless. It was a lot further than I'd remembered.

"You took your time," said Letty.

"Sorry, my purse was right at the bottom of my rucksack so I had to empty everything out. What have you bought?"

"I've got bananas, Kemp's got a six-pack...of mineral water...not muscle." She giggled. "Thomas – I don't know what Thomas has got. He's disappeared. He couldn't make up his mind so I left him to it before I felt the need to strangle him."

"I think I might buy some fresh bread, then we could make banana sandwiches," I said, eyeing up the freshest loaves. I suddenly missed my mum's home-made ones, which was annoying considering it was only my first day without her.

Letty looked blank. Perhaps she wasn't a banana sandwich person.

As I paid at the till, I spotted Thomas. "What have you got?" I asked.

"These," he said with an enormous grin, pulling out a pack of pork cocktail sausages.

"Are you mad?" snapped Kemp. "Magaecians don't eat the flesh of others. You can't bring those."

"You'll have to leave them here," I said.

"But I've just bought them. I'm not wasting them."

"Thomas...you heard Kemp. You can't bring them back," said Letty, looking towards Kemp with a smile.

"Then I'll eat them on the way. I can't eat the whole packet, though. You'll all have to help me."

"Count me out," snapped Kemp, contempt wrapped around each word.

"All right…give us a couple, then," said Letty, holding out her hand.

He passed a number of the little sausages across to me too and we munched our way through the packet before reaching the Tribourne Hotel entrance.

"You'll need to hide the wrappings," said Kemp, his voice tight and trembly, which made me feel as though we'd be in serious trouble if we didn't.

"Where?" said Thomas with a mouthful. He'd managed to make his fingers all greasy and sticky and wiped them on his trousers, leaving a noticeable stain.

"Here," I said, taking the packet. "I'll shove it in the bushes. No one will know."

My friends agreed and walked quickly up the Tribourne Hotel path to meet the rest of the school, who were relaxing on the grass verges, chatting and gossiping on old benches in the overgrown grounds. A selection of appetising sandwiches and other food was beautifully laid on a large, antique wooden table. I didn't bother to investigate as I was feeling quite nauseous from my overindulgence of sausages. Thomas managed to pick up a couple of sandwiches, offering them up to us, but I could tell by Letty's wave of rejection that she must have been feeling a bit sick too. The tall, willowy figure of Fenwick Barclay strode over to inform us that it was time to return to the tutor room. When we arrived, some of the class were sniggering. Orford Nibley-Soames looked particularly irate as he glanced up at the spell written in neon yellow marker on the wall. It read:

*Sh***OUT PLISKY** *not Nash* **TRASH!**

"What's going on?" bellowed Myerscough, who had just entered the room and caused practically everyone in it to jump. Utter silence filled the air as Myerscough scanned for the guilty subject in the direction of the only three *pliskies* in the vicinity. He then snatched my rucksack to observe the graffiti in neon yellow.

"I see," he said, then grunted. "Let's clarify things from the start, boys and girls. A true Magaecian needs patience to learn…integrity…" As he spoke, he unrolled a very large make-do white board which was like a large blank sheet of paper. He detached the backing to stick it quite expertly on the wall over the neon writing. Picking up the yellow marker, he began writing on the sheet as he spoke. "A true Magaecian needs strength to know no prejudice, and most importantly a true Magaecian will never yield to injustice." As he stepped away, it was clear what he'd written…

P atience
L earn
I ntegrity
S trength
K now no prejudice
Y ield NOT to injustice

"I didn't realise it meant that," said Aldwyn Garrick in surprise.

"It *doesn't*," replied Nibley-Soames sharply.

Nyle bravely picked up the marker now abandoned by Myerscough and wrote PLISKY on his bag. "It's a good spell…a really good spell. Anyone else?" he continued, looking my way with a grin as he held up the pen in defiance for anyone fearless enough to accept.

"Give it here," said Delia, who was surprisingly not the only one. From a class of eighteen, almost half now had PLISKY on their rucksacks.

"I was right. You're going to be nothing but trouble," mumbled Myerscough with a shake of his head.

"Like my father?" I asked with a grin.

"No!"

I stopped grinning.

5

USING A KNIFE AND PORK

"In Year 8, we divide you into three groups…in this case, six pupils in each group," started Myerscough. "This makes it safer to keep an eye on you. At the end of each travelling day, all three groups meet up and we discuss what we've learned that day." He looked extremely stern as he read out the first six names. "Orford Nibley-Soames, Vikesh Panicker, Ainsley Hamilton, Imogen Barlow, Retha Magoro and Paige Livingstone. You six go with Mrs Hayhurst, please."

I heaved a sigh of relief at not hearing my name in a group with the obnoxious Orford Nibley-Soames.

"Why is Myerscough always in such a bad mood?" asked Letty.

"You'd be in a permanently bad mood too if you'd been tortured by Nash and his men," said Kemp as quietly as he could.

"Really? Tortured?" said Letty, sweeping her hair behind her ears in a provocative manner, which couldn't be overlooked by Kemp, who was turning red.

"For weeks…so they say," added Nyle.

"Tortured for what?" I asked.

"Tortured for the whereabouts of Nash's girlfriend, of course. Nearly killed him. He is seriously tough, that man… seriously tough."

"But why would he know where Nash's girlfriend might be?" I asked.

"Because he was Darwin Burgess's closest, most loyal friend – and Nash's girlfriend…well…she was Burgess's sister. No one knows what really happened to her. They say Nash never found her but some think he did…and must have killed her."

"So Nash's girlfriend wasn't Magaecian-born?" I asked, shocked at this new revelation.

"Letty Keel, Kemp Barclay, Nyle Pinkerton, Delia Wu, Thomas Marks and Ellery Brown – you're with me."

"Should be *fun*," said Letty, raising her eyebrows sarcastically.

"Prisha Kapoor, Averil Harrington, Angela Yin, Lawson Oakes, Aldwyn Garrick and Teddy Wade – go with Mr Ademola, please."

Our group of six stayed in the room among the musical instruments while the two other groups set off on their afternoon excursion.

"Will we be taking any of the instruments, sir?" asked Delia.

"Not for this short excursion…but we'll choose one or two for our peregrination later."

"Why?" Letty's question was meant to be whispered to me in secret but instead came out rather loudly by mistake.

"Because, Miss Keel, music is important in life. It creates a universal spell. There's an 'us' in music which unites the living with incredible force to form an inexplicable magic. It reaches the unreachable. Music is the only thing which can enter the heart to alter the mind."

Letty stood silent.

"There's also a 'sic' in music," whispered Thomas.

"Which is how I will feel if your jokes don't improve, Mr Marks!" shouted Myerscough. "No need to take rucksacks this afternoon. Just need some water and I'll sort out your snacks. We'll make a picnic from what you've picked up from the shops. Delia…you first," he said, holding out his hand to accept a jar of crunchy peanut butter. "Hmmm. Are you planning to pour it onto people's hands or are you inviting us to shove our fingers in there?"

"Ah, yes. I suppose I didn't think of that…sorry, sir."

"Next," he said to Letty, who handed over her bananas.

"Good. Next…"

Kemp handed over the water, which Myerscough passed round to each person. Nyle had bought some mixed seeds and raisins. I could see Thomas's shoulders rising and falling, breathing rapidly as Myerscough got nearer and nearer to him.

"You haven't eaten your snack already, have you, Sticky?"

"No," I replied quickly. "He forgot his money so he was going to share mine."

Myerscough grunted in his usual fashion as he accepted my bread. Thomas passed a subtle smile in my direction. Kemp, however, was looking even paler than usual.

"You all right?" I asked.

"He knows…about the sausages…he knows."

"No, he doesn't. Relax. It'll be fine."

"Ready?" yelled Myerscough.

We all nodded, then followed the large man, who walked at a brisk pace to exit the classroom towards the grand entrance of the estate. I suspect if we weren't ready, he'd have gone anyway.

"We're heading to a smallholding for some non-human company," he started.

None of us had any idea what he meant.

"My job is to get you to understand your place within this beautiful and quite complex planet. I don't want to see any smart devices. That includes smartphones, laptops, tablets… understand?" He turned around to see us all nodding. "While you may think it makes you more connected to the world, it distracts us from what is actually going on in our immediate surroundings."

I put my hand in my pocket to touch my phone, then removed it quickly as the eyes of Myerscough scorned in my direction.

"Some of you might have experienced trekking in the great outdoors but for others it will be a novelty. Novelty is good…always good. It awakens the senses and this, in turn will lead to new, perhaps unexpected experiences. A surprisingly vast knowledge of chemistry, biology, natural pharmacology, ecology and geology lies within our midst."

"That's a lot of *ologies*," whispered Thomas.

"Don't take my word for it. I want you to experience and discover it for yourselves. Now then…before we leave the estate, close your eyes."

54

It seemed like an odd thing to ask, but no one was going to argue with the grumpy hulk.

"What can you smell, Delia?"

"Grass, sir. Freshly mown grass."

"Yes, indeed – from the land behind the local pub. Sweet and fragrant. Well done. Anything else…Kemp?"

I squinted open one eye to take a peek at Kemp's now crimson complexion.

"Hay, sir?"

"Yes…but remember horses eat a lot of grass so what you might actually be smelling is horse sh…shlop."

I spluttered in my attempt to avoid laughing aloud, which triggered the majority of the class into opening their eyes. Myerscough turned and glared at both me and Letty holding our mouths as we sniggered uncontrollably at his dire attempt to avoid using a more obvious word.

"Horse manure, for goodness' sake," he continued. "Good. You might as well keep your eyes open now. What about you, Sticky? Smell anything?"

I wished he'd stop calling him that. It was unnecessary and just downright rude, if you asked me.

"Coffee?"

Myerscough nodded with a chuckle. "At least you didn't say sausages."

Kemp and I immediately caught each other's eye. Poor Kemp looked as though he might stop breathing. As we set off through the gates, Myerscough signalled for Thomas to walk ahead with him.

"Told you," whispered Kemp.

However, the beaming smile on Thomas's face told a

different story completely.

"What did he say to you?" I asked.

"He said I could have a *blue* on the rainbow system…for standing up to Nibley-Soames in order to protect my friend."

"You mean, when he was going to punch me?"

Thomas nodded, then added, "I'm not really sure what a *blue* means. I'm not actually sure what the whole rainbow system means. Do you know?"

"It's easy," said Nyle, moving forward from behind me. "We all start in the middle of the rainbow on green, which is worth fifty points. A blue is worth plus twenty points; indigo is plus thirty and violet is plus fifty. On the other side, a yellow's worth minus twenty; orange is minus thirty and red is minus fifty. You can get a number of points in between… then at the end of the term, the staff take an average and you should be somewhere on the rainbow, preferably green or above and not red or worse."

"What's worse?" I asked.

"You're not meant to end up with minus points but if you do, then anything below a red means automatic expulsion, I suppose."

My heart rate increased uncomfortably. I'd been given a yellow so I was down twenty points already.

We walked for quite a while and I lost track of time and my surroundings. All I could focus on was how difficult it was going to be not to get expelled before the end of my first term…my first week even.

"Stop, class!" shouted Myerscough. "Have a sit-down somewhere and take some water, then close your eyes and breathe deeply."

Letty had already started to sketch the beautiful trees and autumnal leaves swaying precariously on the branches.

"Nyle...any difference in smells?"

"Yes, sir. I can smell poo, sir."

Everyone started laughing.

"Don't you mean *shlop*?" I shouted spontaneously with a giggle until Myerscough's angry expression immediately urged me to hold my breath and bite my lips together in silence.

"Is it a pig farm ahead, sir?" said Nyle quickly, before Myerscough had a chance to take any more points from my rainbow.

"Good lad. It's more of a pig sanctuary, actually. Pigs make good companions, you know. Very bright and loving creatures...seriously mistreated, unfortunately. Ellery...tell me about the landscape we've been through, please."

I hadn't a clue. I wasn't paying attention, thinking only of trying to avoid a red on my rainbow, which I'd probably receive now for not paying attention.

"Nothing? Come on. If you switch off in this game...it's game over. What about you, Letty?"

Letty jumped on hearing her name pronounced with such a bark. "There was a sheep field, sir...lined with beech trees. It was on that hill...quite far away now."

"Good...very good, Letty."

I had to admit, it was pretty impressive. I hadn't noticed any of those things. There was just a hint of a smile from Myerscough, which was a bit of a revelation in itself.

"Our natural environment is like a family household," started Myerscough, who was looking in my direction. "If, for example, we were going to visit Letty's mother…we know that it's very likely that her father would be there also. It's the same with nature. Letty saw beech trees because we were walking on a chalk hill. Beech trees love alkaline conditions and dry soil which is why we'd be unlikely to see many alder trees as they like the opposite conditions. You have to learn to piece things together to slowly build a picture of your surroundings, together with the animals you might encounter within it."

Myerscough handed round some blank paper and HB pencils. "Draw what you see," he said. "You'll see much more than you think when you try to draw it…even if your drawing skills are poor," he added after a while, looking over at Thomas's lousy picture.

When we set off again, I made sure I took in every landmark, smell and colour, which was exhausting and a bit overwhelming. Myerscough shepherded us in the direction of the entrance to *Beech Hill Farm*. I'd always associated farms with the smell of animal poo and maggots and was expecting to gag as soon as I entered. I held my breath in the hope that I wouldn't throw up all over my friends.

"What's up?" asked Letty. "Your face has gone all red and weird."

I let go of my breath, pleasantly surprised by the lack of puke-activating fragrances. In fact, although it still smelled a bit like a zoo, it wasn't in any way nasty. A ruddy-faced farmer welcomed us in and led us to the rest of the students from Year 8. They were tucking into a well-earned early tea around some wooden tables and chairs in the farm's courtyard. As our group found some empty seats, Thomas started giggling. A pig nudged at his thigh for some food, then placed its head on Thomas's lap.

"That's Kessie. I think she likes you, Sticky." Myerscough laughed.

Kessie, it seemed, liked everyone and took it in turns to nuzzle up to us until she received food scraps. She then moved onto the next table to repeat the exercise. It reminded me of Lionel, and a sudden pang of homesickness caused me to temporarily lose my appetite.

"Do you think that's what Myerscough meant by *non-human* company?" asked Letty.

"Maybe," I answered.

Although it had been a lovely afternoon walking to the farm, it was good to let our guard down for a bit and relax from Myerscough who had been persistently firing questions at us.

"You four," growled Myerscough, pointing to me, Letty, Thomas and Kemp. "Come with me." He had a large shotgun in his hand, which he hung over his shoulder by a thick black strap. Kemp turned ghostly white and looked as though he might suffer a stroke; Thomas was oblivious to everything; Letty swallowed hard, probably fearing the worst, and I could only imagine that he was going to take us somewhere to shoot us.

"You can bring Kessie," he added.

I felt slightly less afraid to have our porky friend for company and followed with the other three into a small, wooded area.

"Okay…" said Myerscough, cocking back his rifle, then handing it to Thomas. "Used a gun before, Sticky?"

"No, sir," he replied.

"Nothing to it, really. Just do what I say…but be careful when you fire though, as it rebounds."

"What?"

"Aim it right between her eyes for minimum suffering," he said, pointing the gun in Thomas's now violently shaking hands towards Kessie.

"W…w…wwhat do you mean?' Thomas stuttered.

"One shot. It's all you need, boy. Come on!"

"I'm not shooting Kessie."

"Why not?"

"I can't. I mean…I won't shoot her…"

"Really?" said Myerscough, snatching the gun away. "So you can let someone else kill your food for you but you can't kill it yourself? You do like pork, don't you? Those cocktail sausages were full of countless Kessies. I don't suppose you even know how those pigs were slaughtered…where they came from…how well they were or weren't looked after? Are you really that disassociated from what you put into your mouth?" Myerscough was now aiming the gun at the defenceless pig.

"No!" screamed Thomas, launching himself at the pig to cover her with his own body. He squeezed her so tightly I thought he might suffocate her.

"Wait!" I shouted, my voice so high and tight, it wasn't a shout at all. "Wait…please…" I stood in front of Thomas and the gun barrel. My body shook so severely it took all my strength to remain upright. "Magaecians respect all creatures on Magae. That's what you told me, sir. That's what you said." My heart beat so hard and so fast it echoed in my ears.

"Respect," answered Myerscough. "If you want to eat another's flesh, then you try hunting and killing it for yourself. At least then you might have the decency to thank it for giving up its life for you. Perhaps you'll see that meat isn't just a box of funny-shaped food. It's the skin and muscle of *someone* with a character…with feeling…able to experience pain like you or you…or you…or you…"

"I get it!" cried Thomas. "Please don't hurt her. I get it… and I'm sorry," he sobbed, hugging the pig.

"You!" shouted Myerscough to Kemp. "I blame you."

"No, sir," whispered Letty before clearing her throat. "He told us not to bring the sausages but we chose not to listen. It's our fault…not Kemp's."

"If he told you not to bring them, then he did a very poor job of it and he should have been much more convincing than that. Half-hearted effort, Barclay…that's no excuse."

Kemp looked down and nodded. "Sorry, sir."

Myerscough cocked his gun onto the safety catch, giving a grunt. "Take Kessie back to the farm, please, Kemp. The rest of you are coming on a little trip with me."

As if that outburst wasn't enough. What more could he scare us with?

Myerscough drove the three of us for about half an hour in his old, muddy Land Rover jeep which, incidentally, was freezing. He kept his window open the whole time and none of us had the courage to ask him to close it.

"Where are we?" I whispered to Letty through chattering teeth.

Letty pointed to a sign that read: Lawson's Abattoir – *Meating* your requirements since 1951.

"What's an abattoir?" asked Thomas with a naive smile.

"That man's not going to let it go, is he?" said Letty.

Before I had a chance to answer Thomas's question, a short, quite dumpy man came to the jeep to greet us. I was guessing he was too young to be *the* Mr Lawson but instead might've been a descendant of the great, possibly late Mr Lawson on the sign.

"Hendrick, my man," he said, shaking Myerscough's hand through the open window which was practically swallowed up by Myerscough's enormous fist.

"Desmond," he returned.

The jovial man peered through to the back where the three of us sat silently like lambs to the slaughter, for want of a better analogy. "Bit young, aren't they?" he added.

"Never too young, Des."

Letty closed her eyes, dropping a couple of tearful plops onto her lap.

"Don't worry," I said. "It'll be fine. I mean, how bad can it be?"

She glared at me, knowing full well that this was Myerscough we were talking about. It was going to be as bad as it possibly could be.

"We'll get through it, Letty. I promise."

She wiped her cheeks and nodded.

"This way," sang Desmond, obviously enjoying his new visitors. "You'll need to dress appropriately."

He led us to a room where we found black wellington boots of various sizes, none of which were small enough for Letty or me; white, stained overalls smelling of bleach; a hair net which made Thomas look like a girl but didn't have the same effect on Myerscough, who appeared even more threatening than usual. There were also white, shiny hard hats which again were a couple of sizes too big for us girls but not a problem for Thomas.

"Why do you think we need the hats?" asked Letty.

I had absolutely no idea and just shrugged.

"Lots of hooks and very heavy dead meat above your heads," answered Desmond, wide-eyed with excitement.

All dressed up in our abattoir gear and looking pretty ridiculous, Desmond led us through some enormous doors. We were immediately hit by the overwhelming smell of disinfectant, coupled with the uncomfortably arctic temperature within the room.

"Silence from here on, please. No more talking now," said Desmond, pressing his finger to his lips. The eerie silence only highlighted the horror of the swaying dead bodies above our heads. Huge beasts hanging undignified by their hind legs. There was no escape from the blood, a shocking red smearing the walls in all directions. I felt as if we'd interrupted a terrible murder. The workers moved quietly, wearing belts containing knives, chinking discordantly in an atmosphere of abomination. Trays of internal organs scattered around the room like some sort of evil experimental lab. Bits of fat hanging above us like decaying frilly curtains an old aunt might have held on to for many years.

"Let's go into the killing room," said Desmond in hushed tones.

I was so traumatised by this point that whatever he said didn't form any type of coherent sentence. I didn't dare look at my friends for fear of allowing my hysteria to surface, which would most likely be contagious. A couple of pigs bounced in, totally oblivious to the horror awaiting but still appearing slightly ambivalent in their uncertainty with their new situation. There were two or three men standing above the pigs. I couldn't really focus as everything surrounding me now seemed to blur into one red and white blancmange of hell.

One of the pigs was gripped with some very large pincers which supplied a lethal electric shock, causing it to fall instantly. Dead. Some naive part of me thought the other pig would be unalarmed by this, unaware of meeting the same terminating situation. It was only a pig…right? But I was wrong…*so wrong*. Pigs are sentient beings, able to feel pain and fear like any person. A glazed look of bewilderment was fast replaced by anguish…sheer terror at the flashing awareness of what was to follow. The poor pig backed up in an attempt to remove itself from its untimely death sentence, but there was nowhere to hide.

I was frozen, my feet turned to stone in the oversized wellie boots. Before I could even open my mouth to shout "Stop!"…to save just one poor animal that didn't want to be killed…it was gone…dead. I felt my heart pumping harder than ever and I couldn't hold back my tears as both pigs were hauled up within a matter of seconds. I was consumed with grief and disappointment – disappointment at not being able to speak up and do something. I didn't, for an instant, expect that all humans would give up pork…but maybe if they saw this, they might not eat as much of it. How much meat do we really need anyway? When I thought the ordeal was over and couldn't get any worse…the man cut the dead animals' throats, instantly releasing a torrent of blood to cover the floor in a foaming crimson wash. The pigs were then skinned and burned before being scalded in boiling water. As I watched the pigs dripping with blood – dark, viscous liquid pooling over their eye sockets while they hung upside down, I saw Letty crash to the floor unconscious. I felt as though I was wading through sticky toffee, my body moving in slow motion towards her. Myerscough dashed to carry Letty away against the unbearable stench of burning skin and other obnoxious odours I'd rather not identify. Myerscough ushered me away to the exit, where I found myself gasping for breath. As I staggered, I lost my footing in the enormous boots, falling head first with quite a bang, displacing my hard hat to slide over my face. I didn't try to move, I just remained still in an attempt not to suffocate or vomit…whichever came first. I lay on the ground in a dazed state of upsetting confusion until Myerscough's deep voice told me to sit upright.

"Too much?" Desmond laughed. "They're all killed humanely. There's no better end for them, you know. Far better than dying painfully in the wild."

I disagreed. In fact, I couldn't disagree more. How could this possibly be better? Mum was always banging on about animal welfare. The number of times she'd caught me tutting or rolling my eyes during her *lectures*…but she was right all along. I'd rather take my chances in the wild, hunted down by a big cat that delivered a deadly bite to the neck with vice-like jaws around my throat. Even if it took minutes rather than seconds to die, it had to be better than death by Lawson's Abattoir…anything but death in here…

anything. Myerscough offered his hand to help me up but my hand was shaking so much, I couldn't grip him. Thomas had apparently thrown up quite near the beginning of the tour. I doubt he'd touch another cocktail sausage ever again.

We retuned all our gear and left almost in silence. I think Myerscough must have said something to the jubilant Desmond Lawson who, I think, found the whole distressing episode highly amusing. I'd switched off, wanting nothing more than to get as far away from here as possible – and as quickly as possible. We strapped ourselves into Myerscough's jeep, Letty in the front so he could keep an eye on her, then set off back to Tribourne. Myerscough said nothing. His stony expression was almost inhuman. Letty was quite clearly in shock and needed some attention. Myerscough pulled over and reached down to produce a shiny silver flask. He opened it and poured out a steaming cup of something. I couldn't identify the aroma as I could still smell pig poo and blood. I wasn't sure I'd ever smell anything else again.

"It's hot chocolate. Dr Ramsay made it for me…for medicinal purposes. Here…drink some." He passed it to Letty but she was catatonic. He held it to her lips, making her sip slowly, then she took the cup in her hands, continuing to drink on her own.

"Better?"

Letty nodded, dropping tears every time she blinked. "Thank you," she croaked as she returned the cup to Myerscough. He refilled it, then passed it back to Thomas, who looked dreadful. I was so angry. Why would anyone expose children…adults, for that matter, to something like that?

"What kind of a teacher are you?" I said, punching Myerscough in the back. He turned to face me so quickly that I thought he might bite me.

"I told you from the start…never take another's word for it…experience it for yourself. You can't tell me you didn't learn something new today…barbaric though it was?"

I didn't answer.

"Eating flesh comes at a price. It's a dreadful business, Ellery. I wanted you to see how you got your finished product. In fact, if I'm honest, most abattoirs are not like Lawson's…they're far, far worse. Animals treated as though pain is of little consequence as they're put through an animal concentration camp. Never take things for granted. *Know*…then come to an intelligent decision as a result of your knowledge. Ignorance should never be an excuse. Just because you don't see it doesn't mean it doesn't happen."

"Is this why Nash hates us?" I asked.

"Partly."

"But if we stopped eating meat," said Thomas, "then what would happen to all the animals? Would they rise up against us and take over Magae?"

"No, of course not…but it would prompt the livestock business to reduce the number of female animals they inseminate."

Thomas looked confused.

"Make pregnant," I explained, which resulted in a knowing nod from Thomas.

"It's supply and demand, you see. If we don't demand as much meat, then they won't need to supply as much."

Thomas nodded again.

"The obscene amount of animal feed grains we produce will be reduced, resulting in less deforestation and less pollution." Myerscough peered in his mirror, probably to check Thomas and I were listening. He scratched his stubbly chin before continuing.

"This means we'll be able to produce more food for those who are starving, and we'll have more land for returning habitats to wildlife that has been depleted by growing grains to feed livestock."

Thomas shrugged at me.

"Streams will run clearer," continued Myerscough, obviously struggling to make his explanation *run clearer*. "It means more birds, more aquatic life, less pesticides and fertilisers, so the condition of oceans will improve. Global warming owes a lot of its blame to livestock producing dangerously high amounts of methane into the atmosphere."

Thomas appeared to have more colour back in his cheeks as he listened intently to Myerscough's wise words. "Do you mean cow farts?" He giggled.

"Yes…and cow burps. It's not something that will be fixed overnight but Dwellers need to be taught how to break from their deeply ingrained habits, so that one day, eating meat will become as odd as eating people."

Thomas looked at me, covering his mouth after letting out a little giggle, which turned into a spluttery fart noise against the palm of his hand.

"Magaecians are vegans." Myerscough sighed. "In one day, just one Magaecian can save three square metres of forest, twenty kilos of grain and over five thousand litres of water. Did you know that one fast-food burger is equivalent to two months of showering?"

We shook our heads like a couple of those nodding dogs you get on car dashboards.

"And of course, if you're an animal lover then every single day an animal's life can be spared from suffering. Becoming a vegan may be a bit too drastic for a Dweller but eating less meat is not impossible…and everyone needs to, before it's too late."

"Why doesn't anyone in Tribourne know this?" I said. "You'd think the village was still living in olden times, before there was internet. I mean, everyone knows that we should shower more and bath less to save water; and remember to turn off the lights to save electricity. Even our teachers at Saint Timothy's told us we should walk to school if we could. So why does everyone here eat so much meat if it's such a large part of global warming?"

"Why indeed," mumbled Myerscough under his breath.

As we pulled into the estate of the Tribourne Hotel, Letty had fallen asleep. I'm not sure I'd be able to sleep tonight, or ever, after what I'd just witnessed. As Myerscough unbuckled Letty and carried her from the front of the jeep, he dropped his wallet, which fell open onto the gravel. A cracked photograph of two young, muddy-faced boys smiled back at me. One was definitely a youthful Myerscough but the other was not familiar. I'd remember a face like that… carved and beautiful. It was the type of face you'd see as a portrait painting hanging in a posh art gallery, unusual but striking and a touch bewitching.

"Put it back in my pocket, please."

I did as I was told – no questions asked, then followed Myerscough inside with Thomas trailing silently behind me. It had been a terrible day…an unforgettable, possibly even enlightening but absolutely terrible day. A light supper had been set up for us but I couldn't face any food so headed straight for the assembly hall covered with soft cushioned sleeping bags. Although I thought I'd never sleep, I was overcome with exhaustion and slipped into unconsciousness within seconds of my head hitting the pillow.

6

THE EBONOID

I was woken by a soft, tickling snout in my ear. "Kessie?"

"She's ours," said Thomas. "To keep. To take on our trip. Isn't it great?"

I sat up and rubbed the sleep from my eyes. I felt an uncomfortable apprehension at what might lie ahead. If every day were to be like yesterday, I'd probably be dead before the weekend. Either that or locked up somewhere for becoming a raving loony, or more appropriately, a vegan fruitcake!

"Breakfaaaaast!" sang out a loud baritone. It wasn't Myerscough but I did recognise the voice to belong to Mr Ademola, a much more affable character. I'd slept with my watch on and almost had a fit when I saw it was only five thirty in the morning. Who in their right mind gets up now? And why did everyone seem so bright and happy about it? I reluctantly got washed and dressed then headed towards the sound of clinking cups and crockery.

Already seated at a large, round table were Nyle and Kemp, Angela Yin, Teddy Wade, and Letty who was summoning me and Thomas to grab the last empty seats beside her. The dreadful smell of yesterday was replaced with the glorious aroma of pancakes and maple syrup. A beautiful display of colourful fruits accompanied the treats as well as porridge and hot chocolate in various flavours concocted by Dr Ramsay. There was hot chilli chocolate…a bright yellow turmeric version…original dark, and an icy cold frothy choconana shake made with plant milk.

"What's this?" I asked, picking up a slice of fruit loaf.

"It's *donk*," said Nyle. "Magaecian bread. Good with peanut butter… Here," he said, buttering a piece and passing it over.

It was so good. Comforting somehow, sweet and gooey. "Why is it called donk?" I asked with a giggle. Let's face it, it was a funny name.

"I think it's a slang word for a car engine. Donk is what your body needs to work its engine, I suppose. We learn how to make it on our peregrination…although most of us already know."

"It's really easy," said Delia, who had just squeezed onto a seat with Angela. "My mum puts banana in hers."

"We wondered where you went yesterday," said Nyle, changing the subject. "Kemp told us what happened. What was it like…at Lawson's?"

Letty's eyes became watery as she sipped at her hot chocolate.

"Whatever the opposite to *totally Hawk* is…that's what

it was…only more," I mumbled with a large bite of donk. "Let's just say…there is no laughter in the word slaughter."

"Good one," said Nyle with a laugh, raising his glass of chocolate plant milk in my direction.

"What?" added Thomas, accidentally spitting out a mouthful of half-chewed food over the table. "I don't get it," he continued, wiping it away with his sleeve.

I wasn't in the mood to explain it to him.

"Myerscough's off his head," said Vikesh Panicker, who reached over me to grab practically the whole plate of donk. "No wonder he never found a girlfriend." He then accidentally nudged Thomas in the back, making him spill his choconana shake all over the place.

"What's that meant to mean?" I asked as I passed a wad of serviettes to Thomas.

"Apparently," said Delia, finishing her drink, "they say that when Darwin Burgess was killed," she switched to whispered tones, "it was Myerscough who saved his sister, Nell Burgess, and hid her. That's why Nash captured and tortured him…to find out where she was. But he never yielded. He's hard, that man. My mum thought Myerscough might've been in love with her."

"Really? In love with Nash's girlfriend?" I found it difficult to imagine Myerscough being in love with anyone. Letty had obviously stopped listening as she was arranging her fruit, trance-like, into a rainbowesque masterpiece.

"How did Nash kill him? I mean…Darwin Burgess?" I asked.

"How are we doing this morning, younglings?" broke in Myerscough, uncharacteristically cheerful, before I'd managed to get my answer. "I need a word, please," he said, summoning me with a flick of his large hand. Letty started crying again but it was only me that he'd summoned so I suppose I should have been the one crying, not her.

"Yes, sir!" I shouted with an army salute and a Gestapo click of my heels.

Myerscough showed no emotion so I lowered my hand quickly from the side of my head.

"Dr Ramsay informed me of an outburst at the end of her class yesterday…with Master Nibley-Soames?"

I didn't answer but just looked down.

"I made a promise to your mother to look after you, Ellery, but I don't expect to act as your personal nursemaid. You need to know how to control that temper of yours and do your mother proud. She's worked very hard to bring you up on her own. How do you think she'd have felt at your outburst yesterday?"

"Why should Nibley-Soames be allowed to do or say whatever he likes just because his parents are best mates with Nash? Why am I in the wrong here?"

"Answer my question, please."

I stood indignant, pursing my lips and clenching my fists.

"Answer me!" he hollered, making me jump. Pupils' heads turned away from their breakfasts to gaze in the direction of the commotion Myerscough was creating.

"Ashamed?" I whispered.

"What? Speak up."

"Ashamed," I repeated, feeling my chin quiver but doing my utmost not to release any tears as I bit my lower lip. He handed me a tissue as if it were the norm to make everyone in his presence cry. He then turned his back on me to focus his attention on a teacher I'd not seen before.

"Mr Mitchell!" he called out before swivelling his head back to me. "Keep that temper to yourself, Brown. Understood?"

"Yes, sir," I sniffed, but in truth, I still didn't see it as a problem. I was only sticking up for myself and I wasn't about to let someone like Nibley-Soames walk all over me.

Mr Mitchell, an athletic-looking, dark-skinned man, acknowledged Myerscough and strode towards him. His jet-black hair was tied neatly into two shoulder-length plaits either side of his middle parting and he'd entwined a small white feather into the end of one of them. I was so fascinated by this man that I felt compelled to eavesdrop on his conversation with Myerscough just to hear his voice, so I bent down, pretending to tighten my shoelace.

"Good to see you, Hendrick," said Mitchell with a distinct American twang.

"And you, Hakan. How's Laura and the kids?"

"All great, thanks. So, my friend, any bright sparks among the new Year 8s?"

Myerscough grunted.

"There must be one or two individuals to note, surely?"

I looked up from my pretend shoelace tightening, to see Myerscough about to turn round. I sprang across the floor, just in time to avoid his gaze, landing behind a large basket of apples. I stayed crouched, doing my best not to make a sound.

"I guess they're quite a lively lot. Could be challenging."
"How so?"

"I'm starting to suspect that one of the younglings might be…an ebonoid," murmured Myerscough faintly.

"Whoa! An ebonoid? Are you sure?"

"Not completely."

"You've seen evidence?"

There was no answer and not wanting to draw attention to my eavesdropping, I didn't look round the basket of apples to see if Myerscough had nodded.

"There aren't many of those around. In fact, I haven't come across one since school…since…"

"Since Nash. Yeah, I know."

"Does your youngling know?"

"Not a clue."

"I see. Let's discuss it over a coffee. I could do with one right now." Mitchell laughed as he led Myerscough to the other side of the room.

I went back to sit with my friends and took one more slice of donk.

"What did he want?" asked Letty, her face twitching.

"Who?"

"Myerscough, of course."

"Oh, yeah. Nothing much. Just told me off for yesterday with Nibley-Soames."

"You look miles away, Ellery. What are you thinking?" said Nyle with a cheeky grin as if he had me sussed.

"What's an ebonoid?"

The table was instantly silent and all eyes looked my way.

"Why do you ask that?" snapped Nyle.

"Because we've got one in our year," I answered, still oblivious to what it meant.

76

"How do you know?" squealed Delia.

"I overheard Myerscough talking to Mr Mitchell."

Thomas seemed disinterested, too engrossed with his breakfast, most of which was all over his hands and face, but Letty had pricked up her ears, obviously as curious as I was. The rest of the table, however, looked horrified. Kemp had turned pale.

"So what does it mean?" I asked. "What's an ebonoid?"

"Shhhh!" Kemp retorted angrily.

"Some of the great Magaecian masters have been ebonoid," began Delia. "Certainly, through history there have been one or two…but they're extremely rare."

"But what are they?" asked Letty as if she'd burst if she didn't find out in the next five seconds.

"It's a person with negative energy," continued Delia. "We all have negative energy but an ebonoid has the ability to physically produce it. The term stems from the word *ebony* which is a dark black wood. It's normally associated with a form of dark or black Magaec…using Magae's natural energy in the darkest ways. It's a powerful force that's very difficult to control. It tends to control *you*. The great Magaecian masters have always channelled negative into positive because there's nothing more powerful against a negative energy than a positive one."

"Then why couldn't Darwin Burgess do it?" I asked.

"He wasn't a natural ebonoid. There really aren't many about. I think it tends to run in family lines. You know? A hereditary thing? We're all able to learn to channel energies, positive and negative, but we don't all have a natural gift to physically produce them at will. Those that do can have a great advantage over those that don't."

"Like Nash. He's one, isn't he?" I said.

"Yes." Delia nodded. "He learned to use his negativity to produce more negativity. My parents say it can only engulf and destroy you in the end – not to mention innocent others that might get in the way. They both say he's never coming back. He's done some terrible things," Delia broke off with a whisper.

"But that's because he thinks there's no other way to save Magaecians," said Teddy Wade. "Not that I'm justifying what he's done or anything…" he added quickly. "But if you see it from his point of view, I suppose he's not all bad. I mean, he's looking out for his people…extreme though it is."

"Are you serious?" screamed Delia with indignation. "You can't go around killing people because they don't agree with you. He killed the head of the Magaecian Circle, for goodness' sake. He was our only hope of ever teaching Dwellers how to respect their planet…our only chance to make things better…to stop Magae from wiping us out. He's short-sighted and a dictator into the bargain. If it's only going to be Magaecians that remain on the planet, do you really think we'd be any better off with Nash in charge?"

"But how can you defend yourself against a power like that?" I asked.

"I'm not sure that you can," said Nyle.

"Maybe this new ebonoid in our year might be taught how," I suggested.

"Ellery…" Kemp decided to have his penny's worth. "Being an ebonoid isn't really a gift anyone wants to have. This person in our year probably won't want anyone to know. It's something that tends to destroy you. I don't think

78

many manage to control it…and more often than not it will end badly, killing you and anyone close to you. Magaecian parents always warn their kids to stay clear of these people. No one wants to be the innocent bystander if a negative energy gets out of hand."

"You can't just decide not to talk to someone because they have an affliction," I retorted. "That's ridiculous."

"I wonder who it is," whispered Teddy before I had a chance to start my debate.

"Finish off now, please," screamed Mr Ademola. "Your journey starts at six thirty prompt. Make sure you pick up your chocolate from Dr Ramsay before you go, please."

7

TOTEMS

Our rucksacks were packed with our overnight stuff, toothbrushes and changes of clothing. Mum had sneaked a new bookmark into one of the side pockets. I loved reading but I didn't want anyone else to know that. I didn't want to be the class nerd. I examined the shiny new bookmark, which had a cute-looking honey badger on one side – even though I knew they were anything but cute – and *Love you always, Mum xxx*, on the back. I shoved it back into the pocket before anyone saw.

My new school uniform was composed of a regulation safari-like tracksuit, which included a khaki polo top, piped with dark green and red on the collar. The Quinton Earth Science School emblem was embroidered on the upper left-hand side of the shirt in dark green. I had matching khaki sweatpants with the same piping down the sides of the outside legs in a stripe, and a pair of hiking boots, which I really liked, especially with my new soft khaki socks. There was also a pair of regulation green wellies which were nowhere to be seen. Delia said they'd been put on the jeep with Mr Mitchell, who was driving to our next school destination. We were to be hiking through some country lanes and woods for most of the morning before catching a train to somewhere near the sea, apparently. I was really excited as the only memory I had of the seaside was when I was really small. It was a day trip to Clacton with Mum. I won a small, orange elephant which I called Phanta.

We had the best fish and chips and then a soft white and very runny ice cream with a large milk-chocolate flake wobbling out of the top. I don't suppose Magaecians were allowed fish…or even ice cream for that matter. I suddenly wasn't feeling as excited as I'd hoped. As I chewed on my nails, I felt an overwhelming wave of homesickness, which was a bit of a shock. All I'd ever wanted was to be a bit independent and be away from Mum's constant worrying and over-parenting and yet, here I was actually missing her, missing home comforts and of course, missing my Lionel.

"You ready, Brown?" barked Myerscough, reminding me that I'd probably need to keep alert for every tree, bush and passing insect as we walked, in case he fired questions at me.

"Fine day to start, younglings," chirped Mrs Hayhurst. She was quite a stout woman. I reckon she could handle a fight with a man-eating tiger if she needed to. Nyle said she was a county shot-putter a few years back, which explained a lot.

We'd been walking for around two hours, hardly saying a word to each other. I felt like I needed more sleep and poor Thomas was looking exhausted. I think he must've been hungry as well. I noticed his chocolatey lips. He'd already started on the slab we made with Dr Ramsay.

"This looks like the place," said Mr Ademola.

As I glanced around me, we were surrounded by trees. They seemed so old and wise that I felt strangely protected here. We continued to walk over the springy moss and fallen leaves, which mingled into a blurry gold and brown plaid. My lungs filled with the freshness of the air, the smell of the earth, the damp wood. A cocktail of life right in front of me and all for free.

Hayhurst and Myerscough nodded in agreement then waved ahead to Mr Mitchell, who must have just arrived. He was carrying a couple of large cooler boxes towards us which he slowly set down in the clearing. He opened the heavy lids to reveal bananas on sticks with a huge ceramic bowl of liquid chocolate for dipping. There were also dates, nuts, almond biscuits, aquafaba meringues, which looked like normal meringues so I'm not sure what aquafaba was…Magaecian donk and flasks of hot chocolate to sip from small coconut shells. These had to be handled with care as some teacher or other had brought them over from his intrepid adventure to Indonesia.

"Okay, Year 8s," said Mrs Hayhurst as she checked her coconut cup for a last drop of chocolate. "Can anyone tell me what that bird over there is…Miss Keel, perhaps?"

"It's a magpie, Miss."

Mrs Hayhurst looked surprised that Letty could identify the bird.

"Yes, it is."

I must admit, my knowledge of bird names was embarrassingly poor but even *I* could've got that one. Mind you, the only other birds I could identify would probably be a robin red breast, a blackbird and maybe a crow. I felt dreadful…I must've seen so many birds every day and yet I didn't know anything about any of them.

"Can you tell me anything about them, Letty?"

"They steal from other birds' nests, don't they, Miss?"

"They are, in fact, scavengers. Very intelligent birds. Highly adaptable and can recognise humans by their faces." Hayhurst then nodded at Vikesh, who had his hand raised.

"The magpie is one of the crow family. People say that they're jack of all trades. They can be predators as well as scavengers and also they get rid of pests."

"Yes, indeed. Well done, Mr Panicker." She smiled then put her finger to her lips. "Listen," she whispered. "Anyone recognise the two-syllable song of the bird in those trees? How about you…Mr Marks?"

It was obvious that Thomas wouldn't have a clue and she knew it. She looked at him mockingly as he sat in ignorant silence.

"Great tit," snarled Nibley-Soames, kicking Thomas in the back.

"All right!" I yelled as I turned round to face him. "Not everyone can recognise birdsong. There's no need to be rude."

The class started laughing.

"Thank you, Miss Brown," said Hayhurst angrily. "In this class we raise our hands to ask or answer questions. We refrain from petty outbursts, which is probably not common practice in Dweller schools. May I remind you…you're not in a Dweller school now, Miss Brown…and here, you lose rainbow points for such behaviour."

I knew it. She was out to get me…and she could. I'd be on orange and only points away from the dreaded red card to be sent off and away from the E.S.S. after only a couple of days. I could feel my face getting hot and my eyes welling up but I did my best to hold back the tears. I didn't want Nibley-Soames to have the pleasure of seeing my distress.

"However, I'll overlook it this once as you're a Dweller and know no better."

Thank goodness for that. Mind you, technically, I was only half-Dweller. My dad was apparently a Magaecian, but I wasn't about to have an argument with Hayhurst after she'd shown me a little mercy.

"The birdsong," she continued, "does, in fact, belong to the great tit, thank you, Mr Nibley-Soames…and well done. Can you tell me a little about the great tit, please?"

"Which one?" replied Orford sarcastically, looking in my direction.

I expected Hayhurst to reprimand him but she didn't. She just smiled, almost encouraging him to continue. I was so angry…but felt like a prize idiot, which is why I chose not to say anything else.

"It's the largest tit in the country…apart from Brown, of course," he whispered intentionally loud enough for everyone to hear. "It's green and yellow but its head is black and its cheeks are white. It's found in woods but it adapts to

84

other areas, often visiting people's gardens. It eats insects, nuts and seeds."

"Excellent, dear. I think that deserves a blue to add to your rainbow."

That meant that Orford's yellow was now cancelled out, which enraged me even more. I could feel my lips tightening and also my stomach, knowing full well I'd have to swallow his obnoxious boasting later.

"Before we set off to London, Mr Mitchell will be teaching your first lesson in totems."

"London?" I whispered to Nyle. "I thought we were going to the seaside."

"They do that a lot now," Nyle whispered back. "It's so that Nash's lot don't follow us and cause trouble. It's safer if no one knows where we are."

I nodded uneasily. What was that meant to mean? What sort of trouble would Nash's lot cause to a load of school kids?

"Welcome everyone," said Mitchell in his dulcet American tones. "Some of you will already know what your animal totem is and some of you may not." He looked across to me and must've instantly recognised the vacant look on my face.

"Of course…you might not know what a totem is. Who would like to explain?" He pointed to Angela Yin, whose hand had flown up immediately.

"A totem is…well…for Magaecians it's usually an animal whose energy is closely connected with their own."

"Good," said Mitchell with a nod. "Once you have discovered your animal totem, you will be able to study as much as you possibly can about it so that you may learn to combine and synthesise with it in order to summon its energy whenever you need it." As he paused, the class was looking particularly excited. I must admit, it did sound really cool even though I wasn't exactly sure what it all meant.

"Try your best to leave your ego behind. Everyone wants their totem to be some sort of glamorous beast like a lion or leopard or maybe even a great eagle…but you must be honest with yourself otherwise your true totem will not reveal itself. The animal chooses the individual…it's not the other way round. There really isn't a *better* or *worse* animal. There are many fine qualities in insects and reptiles so be as open-minded as you possibly can." He passed a pile of large leaves to Myerscough who industriously cut them into small sheets with a penknife. "Take three pieces each and one marker pen from the front, please. We write on these leaves as they may be used to wrap around our totem stones, which we'll be making during our lessons this term. These are banana leaves but some Magaecians use papyrus paper or even cloth. No one need see your writing as the words can be placed directly against your stone. It's between you and your totem…private and personal unless you wish otherwise."

We were all nodding in eager anticipation for our next instruction.

"Okay…on the first slice of leaf, I want you to write down all the animals, large, small, insects, birds etc. that you've encountered recently…in the last week or two."

Everyone wrote feverishly. I, on the other hand, could only think of Lionel. I wrote down dog…then remembered the magpie which I'd seen earlier with the rest of the class.

The ribs of the banana leaves were like the lines of ruled paper so it was quite easy to write in a straight line. After a pause, I could think of a few more animals, in particular a number of crows which I'd seen a few times over the last week. There was also a spider or two, a couple of ants, and of course…the pigs…the dreaded pigs.

"Okay, class…now take your second leaf slice and write down any animal that you have a particular connection with…an animal that really stirs you or excites you or that you just plain like."

This was easy for me. I'd always, always loved elephants and got my mum to collect teapots from anywhere we'd been on holiday as I thought the spouts were like elephants' trunks.

"On your third slice, write any animal you dream about."

I didn't dream about any animals…certainly not that I was aware of anyway.

"You might not dream of animals or might not even realise that you do, which means you need not write anything. Of course, there's always room to write of an animal threat… one you fear…an animal that really, really scares you…even if it's an irrational phobia…you should note it."

I did have a fear…it was of the Asian killer hornet which I'd read about in a *National Geographic* magazine that Mum was sent to put in the school library. As I pondered for a moment, looking at the words on my banana leaf, Nibley-Soames snatched it away and screamed out…"Asian killer hornet? You're not meant to make up your animals from Dweller cartoons, you know. What's an Asian killer hornet? A wasp with chopsticks that does karate?" He started laughing, as did most of the class.

"Whoa, Orford! That's a bit racist...even for you," I retorted angrily.

"I'm not racist. I just hate Dwellers like you who poison the lungs of Magae for greed...by killing off forests to make more room to grow food for the flesh you want to eat. You're putting a death sentence on all of us...not to mention your assault on the oceans. It won't be long before there won't be any fish left. You think it's okay because you walk to school or use fluorescent light bulbs...or you know someone that drives a hybrid car. Global warming's your fault. You've sacrificed our planet for your greed."

I stood red-faced and silent. What could I say? He was right. It was so annoying...but he had a fair point. I swallowed hard. "Okay," I replied quietly through gritted teeth. "I know you're not wrong and I wish I could apologise for all ignorant Dwellers...but that's not the answer. The answer is to teach us. There's still time to educate us..."

"*Educate* you? We need to *eliminate* you...*all* of you...and I'd have no problem starting with you, Brown!"

"I'd like to see you try, Nobbly-Slimes!"

There were gasps among the sniggers but they faded fast as I felt the violent pull on my ponytail as Nibley-Soames pulled my head hard against the ground. I couldn't move. With one hand grabbing his hand on my hair, I used my other hand to grab an opened bottle of water which I'd spotted to my left. I gripped it and flung its contents over Nibley-Soames's face, resulting in his immediate release of my hair. He spluttered and coughed, then started to gulp and wretch. He was gasping for air...choking for breath...

"Move!" screamed Myerscough, barging past me to Nibley-Soames. He made a quick series of odd gestures with his hands to Mitchell, who nodded with urgency.

"What's with the hand stuff?" I asked Kemp.

"Silent spell," he replied. "My brother can do them…but he won't teach me. It's so aggravating…and he knows it."

"It's a bit like sign language," said Letty. "My aunt's profoundly deaf so we all learned how to do it so that we could chat at family get-togethers."

"Really?" said Kemp, obviously impressed.

"What did he say, then?" asked Nyle, unconvinced.

"I'm not exactly sure. I think it was 'take – go?' No, wait…*take* and *get* are the same sign."

"Perhaps it's get a takeaway…like Chinese or maybe pizza," said Thomas, licking his lips.

"Okay, class," declared Mitchell, instructing us to stand up with his hands. "Let's get going and give Orford and Mr Myerscough some room, shall we? Not too far, please."

"That's so impressive," said Kemp, who was smiling broadly at Letty, in admiration.

"Anyone could've guessed that," muttered Nyle under his breath.

"Okay, class. Settle down, please. Mr Nibley-Soames will be fine. Let's continue, shall we?"

Mitchell started rambling on about various famous Magaecians and their totems but I'd switched off by then and my mind started to wonder why Orford had had such a violent reaction to the water I threw at him.

"Welcome back, Orford. Why don't you sit at the front here so that I can keep an eye on you?"

Orford looked pale as he walked to the front of the class with Myerscough, then sat down as directed by the big man. Myerscough pointed to me, summoning me with his thumb in the direction he wanted me to go…which was away from the class for yet another rollicking, no doubt. I looked across to Mitchell, who was making some sort of silent spell to Myerscough.

"Any idea what that means?" I whispered to Letty.

She shrugged. "Go black…or is that white?"

"What?"

"Wait," continued Letty with a pointed finger. "It's easy."

"What's easy?"

"The word's easy. *Go easy*."

"Great. *Go easy*. Should be good. Let me know what I miss."

Letty nodded. "Good luck," she mouthed.

Myerscough led me to a clearing, out of earshot of my class, which could only mean that he intended to shout at me.

"Ellery, which part of this morning's talk did you misunderstand?"

I stood in silence.

"If you can't control your temper then just stay away from this boy. He's dangerous. Don't you see? His father and mother are the closest subjects to Nash, so if you upset their son, you upset *them*, which will put us all in danger, you silly girl."

I tried my best not to cry but I couldn't stop the tears from plunging down my cheeks to drop silently off my face. "I was trying, sir. Didn't you hear me? I agreed with him. I said he was right and that Dwellers had it all wrong. I even came up with the solution…" I cried, in shuddering sobs.

"Calm down. You're hyperventilating."

"But he threatened to *eliminate* me. He was going to kill me!"

"He wasn't going to kill you…but his parents might. These are dangerous people, Ellery. Use your spells. You had him beaten with Nobbly-Slimes."

I stopped crying and smiled.

"I see something special in you, Ellery. Something great that will make a difference in life…but you've got to channel your emotions in the right direction and cast your spells with thought, intelligence and purpose. Do me a favour…stay away from Orford. He's bad news."

I nodded as I took a tissue from his large hand.

"I have a mission for you today. I want you to do something amazing to get twenty points on your rainbow. Get rid of that yellow and do me proud, please."

"Yes, sir," I said with a sniff.

"Now get going."

As I reached my class again, I resumed my seat next to Letty and noticed Mitchell's welcoming smile.

"Okay, class," he continued. "Before we set off for the train, I feel I must quickly revisit the subject of the Asian killer hornet or Vespa velutina or the Japanese Vespa mandarinia which, I'm afraid, are anything but fictitious cartoon characters. They are very real and very frightening and particularly hostile creatures. The queens can grow to the size of your thumb and a swarm can wreak havoc. Not only can they kill a human but also, they rapidly start laying eggs until their hive population reaches about six thousand. To feed their growing larvae they start hunting bees and can destroy an established bee hive in the space of about five minutes. This is bad news…very bad news indeed. Bees are so important on Magae. Do you know why? Ellery?"

"Yes, sir…I think so. We need bees to spread seeds. Without them many crops – like food crops – would die."

"That's right. Bees are pollinators, transferring pollen and seeds from one flower to another, fertilising the plants so that they can produce food as they grow. So, Ellery…what would happen to our food supply without them?"

"I suppose humans wouldn't have much to eat."

"Good girl. Excellent. I think you deserve a blue. Well done."

A blue…that was twenty points…the end of my yellow. I couldn't believe how relieved I felt.

"Well done," whispered Nyle as he tapped me on the shoulder.

"Unfortunately, global warming has something to do with these wasps," continued Mitchell. "Most of the queens would not survive to produce more queens as the cold winters would kill them. However, temperatures have risen enough…maybe just one or so degrees so that they now survive the winters. So…Miss Brown is quite right to fear them. In fact, one might be foolish not to. Have you ever seen one, Ellery?"

"Not in real life, sir. Just in a magazine and in books."

"I see."

"Although…I did have a dream once…when a whole swarm were after me…"

"Really? Did they get you?"

"No, sir. They didn't."

"Good." Mitchell nodded with a smile. "Okay, kids… let's go."

8

QUINTON HOUSE

We took a train to Waterloo, followed by a lousy tube ride to Hampstead Station, all of which we had to stand for. I felt like a sardine. I was hot and agitated, especially as the man behind me had been banging into me with the sharp corners of his briefcase for the last four stops. No matter how many times I squealed or tried to push his case away, he totally ignored me as if it were my fault. He made sure he hit me one more time as he barged past to get in front of me and onto the platform but he stumbled over his own feet, falling embarrassingly flat on his face. Letty and I thought it was hilarious and in my opinion, it served him right but I got a violent tap on the shoulder accompanied by a scornful look from Myerscough, who obviously didn't see the funny side.

It was a short walk from the busy station to Quinton House, a magnificent old, listed building. I'd been to

Hampstead many times – we used to live in London when I was little and Mum still had friends there – but I'd never seen this hidden gem. It was grand in every sense of the word – like Longleat House – with so many windows, only on a much smaller scale and without the safari animals and noise. The sound of chirping birds rose above the low drone of passing traffic. As the whistling breeze caressed my face, I felt strangely privileged to be standing in an area once occupied by noblemen and aristocracy. Myerscough led us through an old creaky wooden gate, so high it made him look short. We followed quietly along a path, unable to miss the beautiful formal lawn to our right, still fairly green, with a neatly trimmed topiary emphasising what a posh place it must have been to live in its day. Chrysanthemums created bright cushions of red, orange and yellow, which finally led on to a sunken rose garden. The distinct scent from the pale pink roses filled the air as if someone had spilled an entire bottle of perfume right in front of me. I couldn't help thinking that roses shouldn't bloom at this time of year but perhaps they were special autumn ones.

"Welcome, welcome, younglings," said Mrs Huckabee, our headmistress, with a radiant smile. "You're all extremely lucky to begin your peregrination here at Quinton House… named after the legendary Scott Quinton, of course. This is a very important building as it was used for hundreds of years as the main meeting house for the Magaecian Circle to discuss Magaecian laws and policies. At the turn of the century the Circle added another part to the property so that they could meet once a month with selected Dwellers, in the hope of putting several policies in place so that Magae might regain her health, so to speak." She was now pointing to the other part of the building. "So…there was now the House of Magaecians and the House of Dwellers. They would meet with regularity, all with supposedly the same Earth sustainability criteria in mind…" She paused for a moment and sighed. "Of course, once Mr Burgess was gone…it was not to be…and the Houses disbanded. The Magaecian Circle still runs, of course, but its whereabouts are unknown to non-members." Mrs Huckabee led us all past some hedges to another garden.

"This is the kitchen garden," she began, looking slightly smug as if she'd planted every tree and shrub herself. "It's a historic orchard containing at least twenty heritage classifications of pears and apples." She signalled for us to put our rucksacks by the door, then we followed her into the building.

We walked down a long ostentatious passageway, passing several rooms on the left and right as we did so. One room contained a plethora of ancient pianos, violins and recorders; another had a collection of oil paintings and tapestries with not much else apart from small, vibrantly coloured stones of all different shapes and sizes, totem stones perhaps but I wasn't sure.

"Here we are…the library," she said with a pleasing smile.

The smell of old paper, decaying and musty, gave me an instant hit of nostalgia as I associated its familiarity with Mum and all the ancient libraries I'd visited with her.

"This is the only library in London with a balcony. You can view the city from here…breathtaking," she said as she opened the set of heavy doors to release a sudden waft of cool air.

It certainly was breathtaking. I could see St Paul's Cathedral and the Shard to my right, and to my left was the unmistakable shape of the Gherkin. In fact, I think I could even see the clock tower at St Pancras station. There was also the immediate green carpet of the Quinton House gardens and a spectacular view over Hampstead Heath.

"Quinton House was donated to our E.S.S. just over a decade ago by the Magaecian Heritage Bureau. It's one of the few permanent E.S.S. buildings," said Mrs Huckabee, ushering us back inside the library, where our rucksacks had magically reappeared. An oldish man dressed like a porter was lurking at the door so I had to surmise no magic was really involved.

"Your totem interviews with Mr Mitchell will begin momentarily and are booked as follows." She read out a list of names and times for us to go individually to discuss our totem animals. "In the meantime, why don't you all find a good book in here. There are no restrictions on any of the books...except the really old and valuable ones, which must not leave the building. We'd rather those particular ones stayed here in the library...but occasionally, you may take them to your rooms. Just make sure you let Mrs Crawford, our librarian, know." She looked across to the tall, skinny woman with dyed black hair and a sallow complexion, who was nodding in agreement.

"Right...who's first?" said Mrs Huckabee, looking down at the list. "Kemp Barclay...come with me, please."

"Yes, Miss," answered Kemp, straightening his polo top, then flattening down his dark, spiky hair.

The library was full of little alcoves containing circular tables at which to sit. Nyle, Letty, Delia and Thomas had found a table together. They had each selected a book while I was still searching for one that didn't look too boring. I looked for ages. The problem was that they were all Magaecian books so I didn't really understand the titles. *Meditative Spells* by I.M. Deep; *Aggressive and Defensive Spells* by N. Vasion, edited by Garry Son; *Auguries Through the Ages* by Horace Cope. I couldn't find anything that looked remotely interesting…until I came across one called *The Ebonoid, Dark and Light* by Raven Lewnie (grand Magaecian Master; Augury [Hons]; author of *Magaeciamatic Solutions*). I took the book to the table to join my friends and sat quietly reading. Kemp had come back and directed Imogen Barlow to Mr Mitchell. He threw his rucksack to the floor and sat gritting his teeth and tapping his fingers angrily on the table.

"How did it go?" asked Letty.

"Don't ask."

"But I did."

Kemp said nothing but just puffed irately.

"C'mon Kemp," said Nyle. "It can't be that bad… surely."

"It's a mouse. My totem's a bloody mouse…not a lion, a man-eating crocodile or even a mysterious scorpion…but a rubbishy, squeaky mouse." Kemp sat upright with his arms crossed.

Nyle put his hand to his mouth to stop himself from giggling.

"So?" replied Letty calmly. "Look at this," she added, turning her book, *Totem Drawings Explained*, to a page with a mouse drawing. "It says the mouse has a gift for paying attention to the smallest details in all that it does. It has a heightened awareness of its surroundings, which means it can spot danger long before others do. The mouse is determined and can adapt. It is focused and grounded, quiet and shy. It has the gift of invisibility and stealth. It is wise and will not overlook the obvious. The mouse relies on good timing, knowing when to do or not to do something. Its greatest power is instinct... regarded with legendary status among other animals. It's the ultimate survivor, Kemp. I mean, wow! If mine's half as good as yours, I'll be more than satisfied."

Kemp looked at Letty and smiled. "Thanks," he said, pushing her book back to her but still looking a bit peeved.

I returned to my book, which was all a bit complicated to comprehend. I continued to read, struggling through the pages until I finally stumbled across a section of interest.

"Whoa!" I uttered aloud, unaware that I'd done so.

"What?" asked Nyle.

I didn't raise my head from my book but continued reading.

"Ellery?"

I looked up, suddenly aware that it was me he was addressing. "Oh...sorry. It's just...well, I think I might know who the ebonoid is."

"Who?" snapped Kemp.

I looked around to check for unwanted listeners. "It's... Orford."

"Orford?" Nyle laughed. "It can't be."

"What makes you think it's Orford?" asked Letty, closing her book on totem drawings.

"It has to be. I mean, Myerscough keeps telling me to keep away from him…he says he's dangerous…"

"And he's right," Kemp replied sharply.

"Look." I turned the book to face my friends. "It says here…immature ebonoid – shouldn't that be ebonoids?"

"The plural of ebonoid is ebonoid…like one sheep, two sheep?" said Delia.

"Oh, right. " I nodded, pausing for a minute. "Anyway… it says that immature ebonoid are unable to control the force that they produce. They may all too often focus it inaccurately on a questionable subject and hit one or more innocent bystanders within the vicinity. However, it is not unusual for a juvenile to have his/her negativity rebound to cause self-injury."

"And?" said Kemp with a bark.

"*And*…the water incident? When he threatened to exterminate me and he pulled my hair. I threw the water over him and he must've wanted to hurt me so badly…but instead of hurting *me*, it rebounded and hurt *him*. He was actually choking…I mean, really choking. I reckon he could've stopped breathing if it weren't for Myerscough's quick response."

Kemp and Letty looked at each other with narrowed eyes, and Nyle and Thomas were silent in contemplation. Delia took the book to examine it further.

"So what do we do?" asked Thomas.

"We try to make him see it our way," I replied. "Once Nash finds out about Nibley-Soames's *gift*, he'll recruit him and force him to use his negativity to make Nash even stronger. We've got to make him see that Nash's way is the wrong way."

"And just how do you propose to do that, Ellery? He hates you with a passion," said Kemp. "Let's face it…he hates all of us."

"I know…I haven't thought it through yet…but I will," I said, taking back the book from Delia.

"Ellery…Mr Mitchell will see you now," said Imogen, pointing me towards Mitchell's room.

"What you're asking," added Kemp wagging his finger, "it's impossible."

"Nothing's impossible," said Letty with a smile.

"Exactly," I returned, closing the book.

"If you're keeping the book, dear…just bleep it out, please," said Mrs Crawford.

I held the book up to a monitor, which registered the book with a bleep. "Don't I need to sign my name or something?" I asked.

"All books have a tracking device. We don't need to know who has the book…only where it is."

I retrieved my rucksack from the doorway and carried the book in my hand, then followed Imogen's directions up the vast spiral staircase, taking a right turn to find Mitchell's office, the first door on the left. I knocked twice and waited.

"Come on in."

I walked into a large, sparsely furnished, whitewashed room.

"Have a seat, Ellery," said Mitchell kindly, pointing to a seat across his desk. At the front of the desk was a collection of stones, large and small, all lined up in a row.

I reluctantly sat down on the red-cushioned chair, which looked like an antique. In fact, it seemed so old and tatty that I thought it might crumble if I sat on it for too long. As Mitchell scribbled my name in his folder, I looked around the room, regarding the few hanging paintings. One portrait in particular, much larger than the others, caught my eye. The subject was an elderly man smiling, his gentle eyes warm and brown and his wrinkled face ruddy and weather-beaten.

"That's Scott Quinton," said Mitchell. He smiled at me then looked at the library book still in my hand. "What are you reading? Anything good?"

I passed the book to him. As he read the cover, he seemed alarmed, his eyes widening. I had an awful feeling that I might be in trouble.

"This is deep stuff, Ellery. Why ebonoid?"

"It's not something I know much about, sir…but I know that Saxon Nash is one…so…I was curious."

"I see," he said, taking a large, steaming mug to his lips. "You don't mind…if I drink this, do you? I'm not going to get a break for ages."

"Of course not," I replied, watching him sip.

Mitchell placed his oversized mug back on the desk, the chocolate aroma filling the room with a pleasing fragrance.

"Sir?" I began meekly, fiddling with my hair. "Why didn't Nash seek help…to control his powers?"

"He did…but unfortunately, he didn't seek the right help. He was taught by a very old Magaecian master who himself was an ebonoid…a distant relative, I believe. It tends to run in families, you know?"

I was nodding, keen to know more. "What happened?"

"Nash killed him. Totally accidental…tragic. You see, two ebonoid together will conflict and repel…like opposite poles. They can't survive together. One has to have full power over the other…so the strongest will prevail, often destroying the weaker one whose ebonoid power will be instantly absorbed by the victor…making him stronger still and more dangerous should he use this negativity with ill nature."

"So how can you beat someone like that?"

"With serious difficulty." He smiled. "Nash needed the teachings of a Magaecian guru not a master and definitely not another ebonoid. A guru teaches control through meditation. The Magaec from an ebonoid works much better when applied upon oneself rather than targeting it against others. So a guru would teach how to channel such energy and control it from within, rather than allowing it out to be directed externally on unsuspecting, unprotected others. He or she would also guide an ebonoid through totem teachings, of course…which brings me…to the real reason you're here, Ellery…to determine your totem. Have you got your banana leaf sections?"

"Yes, sir," I replied, disappointed at Mitchell's decision to stop the ebonoid conversation. I took the three leaf slices out of my rucksack and handed them over for Mitchell to study.

"What do *you* think your totem is?"

"I was hoping it might be an elephant, sir."

"Mmm, possibly. Some people have more than one totem, you know? I have a feeling you might well be one of those people…but for now, I think we'll stick with the pachyderm. Do you know anything about them?"

"They're…big?"

Mitchell laughed. "Yeah…they're big all right. An elephant as a totem will encourage protection, strength and is known to produce very strong bonds with loved ones. They are hugely determined and undeniably loyal. They are steadfast, which means that they are a great energy to call upon in difficult times. It will keep you calm when your path is bumpy and times get tough. The elephant is relaxed unless you mess with her herd…a good force to call upon if you're a bit of a hothead. A quick temper can be a dangerous thing sometimes, Ellery."

I nodded in annoyance, hearing Myerscough's voice coming from Mitchell's mouth, as he'd obviously been discussing me in private.

"I need you to do some homework for me, please. Study and research the qualities of your totem. Find out where it lives, how it moves, feeds, sleeps, adapts to its environment. Read as much as you can about elephants…hang pictures, make drawings…"

"Yes, sir." I nodded.

"To be effective in your life, you must honour your totem's energy. Do you understand?"

"Yes, sir. I think so," I answered, watching Mitchell lean back against the bookcase behind him and pull out a fairly new-looking book.

"Here," he said, passing me *Shapeshifting for Younglings, Book 1*. "Take it…you'll find it interesting."

"Shapeshifting?"

"Yeah…fascinating subject. This one's written by my wife, actually. She teaches it once a week…extremely talented. Have a little read…it might give you a head start over the others."

"Thank you, sir," I replied, placing the book in my rucksack. "Will I be able to change into something else…like an animal or something?"

"You may be able to shapeshift into your totem. This is not necessarily an actual visual metamorphosis but more of a shapeshifting in your imagination...enabling you to see through the eyes of your animal totem. Just because it's not visible in the real world, doesn't mean it's not real."

"Cool." I nodded. I picked up one of the shiny stones on Mitchell's desk. There was a hawk imprinted on it.

"That's my totem stone. You'll learn with Mrs Ball and myself how to make your own one using one of Magae's stones. It has to be a stone that you find yourself. An element that connects you with nature."

I put the stone back as another caught my eye. It didn't have any animal imprinted on it, but was unusual in that it had a hole in the middle of it.

"That's a hag stone," said Mitchell, passing it to me. "Apparently, if you look through the hole, you can see unusual creatures...like fairies."

"I don't believe in fairies, sir. Isn't that for younger kids?"

"Yes, you're probably right. I can't say I've ever really invested in fairies at any age. Of course, some say these stones bring good luck and protect you from negative forces. They're actually naturally occurring stones. Water and other elements batter the stone to eventually create a hole at its weakest point. That's why you often find them near rivers or streams...or maybe even at the seaside. Mind you, if you go looking for one, you'll never find one. They tend to find you." He smiled and held out his hand for its return. "Okay, then. Off you go and tell Aldwyn Garrick to come up next, will you, please?"

"Sure," I said, about to take back the ebonoid book when

Mitchell slammed his hand firmly on top of it before I had a chance to pick it up.

"I'd stick with the shapeshifting for now, Miss Brown. It's much more appropriate for a youngling and far less…heavy. Perhaps you could revisit this one at a later date." He slid open his desk drawer and placed the book carefully inside before slamming it shut.

"But…" I started, ill-inclined to give up the book, but Mitchell's hand was locked tight on the drawer and obviously not going to budge. I pursed my lips in anger, wanting nothing more than to take his hot chocolate and pour it all over his desk. I needed that book to work out a contingency plan should Orford's powers get out of hand. I couldn't wait for the adults to sort it out; grown-ups always took so long to make decisions. It might be too late. Orford needed to be kept as far away from Nash as possible, or Nash would have no alternative but to kill him. Orford would be considered a threat as another ebonoid. Then there was Nash himself with whom I had an unhealthy obsession. He was bound to be somewhere in that book, which was now being held hostage under Mitchell's dark hand. I gave a puff at my frustrating situation and got up from the ancient chair, grabbing my rucksack.

"Damn!" shouted Mitchell, who had spilt his hot drink all over himself.

"You okay, sir?" I asked, watching him pull his wet shirt away from his scalded skin.

"It's fine…just fine. I'll sort it out, thanks, Ellery. You go get Aldwyn for me, please."

"Yes, sir."

9

SHOCKING NEWS

I got back to the library, still frustrated that Mitchell wouldn't let me keep the ebonoid book. My thoughts were interrupted by shouting and screaming between Nyle and Orford, whose overheated conversation was turning into a backstreet slanging match. I looked around for Mrs Crawford but she was conveniently nowhere to be seen.

"What's going on?" I asked Kemp, pulling him back to face me.

"Orford said that Nyle should get a book out on pyrotechnics."

"What?"

"Nyle's dad's been asked to join the Magaecian Circle."

"I don't get it. Isn't that a good thing?"

"No, it's a bad thing. Well…maybe ten years ago it was good, but nowadays it's only Nash's followers on the Circle.

He picks one or two unsuspecting Magaecians so that he can intimidate them and their children."

"Then his dad should say that he doesn't want to join the Circle."

Kemp started laughing. "You're joking, aren't you? Saying no to Saxon Nash isn't an option. You can't say *no*."

"Why not?"

"Because it's Saxon Nash – that's why not. You just don't get it, do you? He makes a poor, vulnerable Magaecian, one with young kids, join the Circle as an act of pledging allegiance to the Magaecian way. To prove that they truly believe in the Magaecian way as opposed to the Dweller way, they must do terrible things for him else he threatens to kill them…all of them saying they're not worthy of the Magaecian name. He gets his cronies to visit members' children and blackmails them into doing terrible things for him, threatening to hurt their parents or some other member of their family in a horrid, gruesome way if they don't."

"What terrible things?"

"You know…like setting Dweller schools on fire… burning down Dweller burger joints…"

"Oh, I see. Does that mean Aiken Thorne's dad is a member?"

"No…not Aiken's dad…but Aiken's mum. Nash probably threatened to hurt his mum or something."

"But that's terrible."

"Of course it is. What would you do if someone threatened to kill your mum in the most agonising way unless you set fire to something or blew someone up?"

I didn't answer. I was brought up to know right from wrong. I couldn't hurt a load of innocent people…but my mum was all I had in the world. There was a sudden *thwack* followed by an *umph* as a fist fight had kicked off between Nyle and Orford.

"Stop them!" I screamed at Kemp and Thomas. "You *must*. Orford could really hurt Nyle if he lets out a negative force."

"Or he could hurt himself if it rebounds like the last time," said Thomas.

"We can't chance it," I cried, barging through the jeering spectators with Kemp and indicating for Thomas to help us remove Nyle from Orford. However, we were beaten by Mr Mitchell, who had quietly forced his way through the class to stand between the boys, catching a punch from either side in each hand. This man was seriously cool.

"Garrick!" he yelled, his American accent far more prominent than usual. "Wait for me in my room for your totem teaching, please."

Aldwyn Garrick sprinted up the stairs while Mitchell glared at me with a look of dissatisfaction.

"What's going on?" he said, enunciating each syllable sternly and assertively.

"Nothing," answered Orford.

"Nothing, *sir*!" screamed Mitchell, causing both boys to jump.

"Nothing, sir," repeated Orford quietly.

"Pinkerton?"

"Just a misunderstanding, sir," he said, wiping his nose and looking daggers at Orford.

"Whatever the misunderstanding, sort it out like human beings and use spells, not fists. You can both have a yellow and you can both write me an essay on misunderstandings and how to resolve them…on my desk by dinner time."

"But, sir…" howled Orford, "I've got Magupe."

"Pardon?"

"Nothing, sir."

"What's Majoopy?" whispered Letty.

"Magusical Physical Education," answered Delia.

"What's Magusical?" I asked.

"You know? Magaecian music…Magusic. Magusical P.E.…Magupe. It's basically exercise through dancing to Magaecian music."

Letty and I nodded and giggled. It was such a funny word, sounding more like a kind of glue than an activity.

"This is the second time you've been involved in an altercation, Mr Nibley-Soames," continued Mitchell. "One more time and you might find yourself being home-schooled."

"I highly doubt that," whispered Kemp. "Not with both parents on the Magaecian Circle."

"Now get out…all of you!" hollered Mitchell.

As we departed in silence from the library, I ran to catch up with Nyle.

"You okay?" I asked, touching his arm.

"Leave me alone," he replied, pulling his arm away sharply.

"Nyle, I only want to help."

"Help? How can you possibly help me? I'm going to have to run for it…hide, in case Nash finds me and makes me do shameful stuff…foul and wicked…"

"You have to say *no*."

"Are you serious, Ellery? No one says *no* to Saxon Nash... not if they want to live."

"Listen, Nyle...Kemp asked me what I'd do if Nash threatened to kill my mum...if I didn't blow up a load of people or set fire to someone's cafe...and I couldn't answer. She's all I've got...I've no one else in the world. Anyway... I've thought about it...and...I know my mum and I know what she'd say. She'd say that she'd rather die a thousand terrible deaths than see me suffer, carrying such anguish and guilt for the rest of my life. She'd want me to say no. If we say no...if we *all* say no, then he'll stop asking. He'll have to find another way to get what he wants...until he's unable to get what he wants because no one will comply and he'll have no choice but to stop. We can't let him terrorise us. He mustn't win like this. This is not the way to put Magae right. If he kills all the Dwellers, do you really believe he'll change when something doesn't go his way? Do you really want to live under a dictatorship, Nyle? You need to say *no*."

"That's easy for you to say. There's only one person you care about...I've got two innocent little sisters and my mum and dad and aunts and uncles and cousins..."

"How can you say that? The fact that I have only one family member makes her all the more precious."

"Ellery, you don't understand. Dwellers aren't like us. It's not my fault your dad walked out on you. Magaecians believe in sticking around for their kids...but you wouldn't understand that. Dwellers don't care about each other like we do. They're different."

"No they're not!" I screamed. I could feel my nostrils flaring as the anger churned in my stomach. "They're not different at all. I hate what my dad did to me and my mum. In fact, I hate my dad. There…I said it. I've never even met him but I know I already hate him. He's never been around for one birthday…never been there to teach me to swim… or ride a bike…he's never even tried to find out what I look like…but most of all I hate him…because he *isn't* a Dweller. He's a goddamn Magaecian!"

Nyle had turned blue in the face and dropped to his knees gasping and heaving, clutching tightly at his throat.

"Nyle?" I broke from my rage and rushed to my friend to help him as he collapsed in a heap, crying out in agony.

"Nyle…I'm sorry, I'm sorry. Please be okay," I cried, smacking away my tears.

"I'll get help," said Letty, who must have come over to find out what the commotion was all about. "You'd better move away from him."

"What? Yeah." I nodded, getting to my feet with my head in a daze. I barged past Mr Ademola who was sprinting to the fallen Nyle.

"Give him room, give him room," shouted Ademola behind me. I didn't turn round to see what was happening but headed instead like an Olympic champion to the remote kitchen garden where I lost control of my sobbing. I stayed there, crying for ages.

"Ellery?"

"Stay away from me, Letty…please."

"Nyle's fine. He's okay…I promise."

"It's not Orford…" I sobbed.

"I know."

"Ellery Brown," growled the unmistakable deep voice of Myerscough, who was signalling with a tilt of his head to go with him.

I sat still, unable to move, hysterically shaking my head in contradiction to his request.

"Go meet your classmates in the kitchen, please, Miss Keel. Chef MacBrennan is teaching Mealish."

"Mealish?"

"Mother Earth, Letty. Mealish, the language of food and food spells."

"Right," she answered with a giggle, then galloped off to the kitchen.

"Ellery," said Myerscough, sitting beside me and passing me a tissue. He seemed to have an endless supply particularly for me.

"I have to leave, sir. I'm dangerous…"

"You don't have to leave…you just need a little help to control this." He put his arm around me and let me cry onto his rock-hard chest.

"But every time I'm angry, I hurt someone," I sobbed.

"Hmmm…but anger isn't always a bad thing, you know. It's an energy – a very strong one in your case, which doesn't necessarily have to be channelled negatively. Your anger seems to stem from injustice. There's nothing wrong with separating right from wrong…so long as you can turn it into a positive outcome by harnessing the energy of your anger. Then, the result can have truly wonderful consequences on an astonishing level, not only for you but also for those around you."

"But I could've killed Nyle. I could've killed…you…"

"Don't flatter yourself. You're not strong enough to kill anyone…especially not me…not at the moment, anyway. However, each episode of negativity will become stronger, which is why Mr Mitchell gave you the shapeshifting book and why you need your totem guiding you. Your temper, more than any other student's here needs the utmost attention…not because it's such a terrible temper…no worse than any other youngling your age, I don't suppose…but being an ebonoid, the powers you may find in black Magaec will give you a false sense of invincibility. You will grow ever more negative as each episode makes you want to continue darker and darker…until you're unable to recognise dark from light. It's at this point that you will not return…and only bad can come of it. Do you understand me?"

I nodded. "No one will want to be my friend now, will they?" I spluttered in between sobs.

"That's bull…ony. A load of baloney," said Myerscough, quickly correcting himself. "You're going to need your friends more than ever now. They will help you as you learn to manipulate your energy in a more positive way. Don't underestimate the power of friendship, Ellery. Tyrants trust very few people and have a scarce number of friends, if any at all. It's a very lonely place to be and because of it, makes them vulnerable. A definite weakness Mr Nash seems to have acquired. His only weakness perhaps…but still a weakness all the same."

I stopped my crying and wiped my face with the tissue before managing a smile in his direction.

"Go find your friends…and stop worrying."

"But—"

"Go!"

"Yes, sir."

"And, Ellery...perhaps it's best not to mention your gift around others yet...not until you've mastered its control. There are many parents who wouldn't take too kindly to their children sharing lessons with a juvenile ebonoid."

"But Nyle already knows, sir...and Letty."

"Yes, perhaps..."

"They won't want to come near me now."

"Ellery, there's an old spell, written by John Churton Collins that goes: *In prosperity our friends know us; in adversity we know our friends.* Think about that. In time you'll see what I mean...and it'll be fine."

"Yes, sir." I nodded but in truth, I hadn't a clue what he was on about. He'd suddenly taken to talking in riddles. I only hoped this wasn't the way he'd choose to continue.

"There's a trick that a good friend of mine taught me for when emotions get out of control. Place your hands together...like someone in a gesture of prayer. When you bring your palms together, all opposite energies meet. Close your eyes and you will feel a small space between the palms. It is here that your self resides between opposing forces...and it is here that you will find a calm and an inner peace. It's a form of namaste...a respectful Indian greeting. It suggests the spirit in you meets the spirit in whomever you are facing. It suggests equality between all...a willingness to share a common ground with all people of all races."

I did as he instructed and found an unexpected feeling

of balance and harmony. I felt…better. It was quite uncanny and not something I'd anticipated.

"Each time you lose your temper, try this pose to remind you to think…not only of the pain you might inflict with your negativity, but to acknowledge that there is always another viewpoint to your own. You must consider the perspective of others. Find what makes you alike rather than what makes you different."

10

COOKING UP A FRIENDSHIP

The kitchen was bustling with students in aprons, collecting ingredients and chopping up vegetables. A wonderful aroma of Indian spices filled the room as children worked to produce a replica of Chef MacBrennan's very professional-looking finished dish. It was the brightest yellow food I'd ever seen.

"Welcome, Ellery. I'm Chef MacBrennan," she said with a broad Irish accent. "We're making *Sunny Curry*, a personal favourite of mine and a very traditional Magaecian dish. Mealish is a major part of Magaecian culture. It's how I met my husband, actually." The short, rosy-cheeked woman chuckled as she pushed a couple of grey curls under her chef's hat and tightened her apron around her ample middle.

"It's so…yellow," I said.

"It is. It's the turmeric. Such beneficial qualities, don't you know."

"Really? Has it?"

"It has…oh yes. It has powerful medicinal properties. It's anti-inflammatory…good for the brain and heart…and plays a part in slowing the ageing process, don't you know," she continued, rubbing at her liny face. I wondered how much linier she'd have been if she hadn't eaten turmeric.

"And then there's the ginger," she continued, now well into her stride. "An old Indian medicine, of course. Good for motion sickness as well. We tend to leave the coriander on the side though because although it's a wonderful herb, it's one of those tastes that you either love or hate."

"Like Marmite?"

"It is," she answered with a giggle. "I, myself, think it's fragrant and fresh…but my husband thinks it tastes of soapy moths. Can't imagine he's ever eaten a moth covered in soap so I'm not sure how he's come to that conclusion. Anyway…"

"Ellery!"

I turned to see Thomas waving at me with bright yellow palms, his smile brightening the room as his face was covered in turmeric. Kemp, on the other hand, was trying his utmost to avoid eye contact. He knew…and if *he* knew, then others might know too. I looked around the room to find Nyle but he seemed unaware of my presence as he busied himself by the stove.

"They'll come around," whispered Letty, who had joined me to help chop the onions.

I smiled and followed the recipe displayed on the board at the front of the kitchen, working industriously with my friend.

"You'll need to wash that face before lunch," yelled Chef MacBrennan in Thomas's direction.

I was grateful for the noisy kitchen atmosphere, still upset that I was the ebonoid and not Orford. I felt light-headed, the tantalising smells were causing my stomach to object loudly with embarrassing growling noises.

I suddenly felt a large hand on my shoulder, which made me jump.

"There's someone to see you," said Myerscough. "Can we have two plates for the dining room alcove, please, Aileen?"

"You can," barked Chef MacBrennan as she hurried around the crockery.

Myerscough led me out of the kitchen throng, carrying two plates of Sunny Curry, then into a much quieter space where I could hear barking. The only animal we had at Quinton House was Kessie and she definitely didn't bark.

"Lionel!" I screamed. "I've missed you so much, boy," I cried, bending down to pick him up and cuddle and kiss him.

"It's only been a couple of days." My mum laughed as she embraced me and Lionel.

"How come you're here? I can manage without you, you know."

"Yes, of course you can," replied Mum, sitting down to eat. "I'm staying with an old friend up in London and I wanted to give you this," she said, handing over a well-wrapped birthday present.

"But it's not till tomorrow."

"I know…but you're apparently setting off on a journey very early in the morning…so I didn't want to miss you. Go on…open it now. You can save the card for tomorrow."

"Okay. Thanks, Mum." I unwrapped the present to reveal a purple square box. "It's beautiful," I said, pulling out a delicate silver chain with a tiny silver elephant charm attached to it.

"Here, let me help you put it on," said Mum.

"It's my totem."

"Yes, I know. Hendrick told me," she said with a smile. "There's a pair of elephant earrings to match."

"Does this mean you can tell me about my dad now?"

"Why would it mean that?"

"Because I'm thirteen. I've a right to know and you're obliged to tell me," I insisted.

"Ellery! You are *only* thirteen, my girl, and I will tell you when I think it's right to tell you."

"It's never right to tell me!" I yelled back at her. I was about to spout out how unfair she was being and what a terrible mother she was when I noticed her grimace and put her hand on her chest.

"Mum? You all right?"

"I'm fine…it's the curry…probably a bit too hot." She smiled.

It wasn't the curry that was too hot, it was my temper. I tried the namaste position and thought about what Myerscough had told me. I felt suddenly calmer and breathed deeply.

"Mum…I'm sorry. I suppose I'm only seeing it from my point of view and not yours. You've probably got your reasons and I should respect that. I've waited this long so I suppose I can wait until you're ready."

"Oh, Ellery, darling…I knew this day would come, just not so soon. I've been dreading it and doing everything possible to put it off, but you're right…it *is* time you knew."

I sat in stunned silence.

"The truth is not a very pleasant one, I'm afraid, so I'd prefer us to be in more familiar territory at home. This is not really a suitable environment. Besides, you have lessons after lunch and I need time to do this properly. I'll make you a deal. If you can keep going until the Christmas holidays, I will tell you what you want to know."

"Everything?"

"Whatever you want to know."

I got up and cuddled her. "Thank you. I know I don't always show it…but I love you, Mum."

"I know…and you're right…you don't always show it." She chuckled.

A hand bell rang loudly for my first afternoon lesson, spells and counter spells with Myerscough.

"You'd better get going," said Mum, fiddling with her serviette. "See you at Christmas, sweetheart. Be alert, be careful, make sure you—"

"Mum! Gotta go."

"You can leave that card with Chef MacBrennan," said Myerscough, who'd come past to say goodbye to my mum, handing her a book entitled *Mealish Made Simple: Food spells for beginners*. Mum looked bewildered but took the pocket-sized book and placed it in her handbag with a nod. Myerscough strode off, leaving me and Mum to have one more hug. Lionel had run off into the kitchen garden so I chased after him for one last cuddle.

I reached Myerscough's room, which had all three groups of Year 8 students sitting in a semicircle in front of our Herculean teacher.

"Okay…settle down, please. This afternoon we will be having a bash at hurtful spells and counter spells."

Delia had a notebook out and neatly wrote out the topic title, underlining it with precision using a bright green biro.

"Spells can cause a great amount of unnecessary pain. Never forget that there is great power in a spell. Unfortunately, once cast, it cannot be uncast…like pulling the trigger of a gun to release bullets which cannot be put back once in flight. However, there are occasions when a particularly nasty spell has been used but a counter spell can soften the blow. Can anyone think of a damaging spell?"

Orford Nibley-Soames's hand shot up.

"Orford?"

Orford turned to Thomas and shouted, "Fat!"

Thomas's face reddened as he looked down at his crossed legs and pretended to smile. Poor Thomas never said a mean thing about anyone. I was furious.

"Weak!" I shouted, looking at Orford. "Boring, uninspiring, dull, screw-up, coward, spineless, flawed, expendable, unnecessary—"

"Ellery!" yelled Myerscough, picking up Vikesh Panicker, who had fainted and was now lying flat on the floor. "You're okay, lad. Just sit still for a moment. Imogen…get me a glass of water, please."

"Yes, sir," replied Imogen, scuttling to the hallway where there were always water jugs.

"I think you misunderstood the exercise, Miss Brown," said Myerscough, assuming the namaste pose.

I reacted instantly by mimicking him.

"I needed a counter spell...for *fat*. Any ideas how you could improve this to be less derogatory?"

"I don't know, sir," I whispered, wiping the tears from my face with my sleeve.

"Why don't you give it a go...please."

I didn't want to but I didn't think Myerscough was allowing me the chance to refuse, so I took a deep breath and began. "Fat...is a complex substance which can be both solid and liquid. I believe a spell to describe the best kind of friend...is a *fat* friend. Someone whose friendship is solid... someone you can always rely on to stick by you, no matter what. Someone who will risk everything to protect you... take a punch for you so you don't get hurt. A fat friend can also adapt to any situation like a liquid that flows around any shape. Even if you turn out to have...an affliction...or an unavoidable genetic flaw, a fat friend will still be there for you. Some people never experience a fat friend so I consider myself extremely lucky in life because I have managed to acquire more than one...and I only hope they think I'm fat too." I parted my hands and breathed out with a puff.

"I hope I'm a fat friend," whispered Letty.

"The fattest." I looked up to see Myerscough nodding in agreement and Nyle acknowledged me with a grin. I looked over to Kemp but he obviously wanted nothing more to do with me and turned away.

***

Despite feeling sapped of all strength, I couldn't sleep. The girls' dormitory was in darkness, quiet as everyone but me was deep in slumber. I was aware of the constant drone of Hampstead's passing traffic, very different from the tranquil stillness of the little village of Tribourne. I also had so many things clouding my mind and all this *trying to keep calm and see the other person's point of view* thing was exhausting me. It seemed to require far too much effort. The thought of having to continue along this path for evermore was not something I was looking forward to. Then there was the niggling question of why Mr Mitchell didn't want me to have that ebonoid book. Perhaps he thought it might scare me too much… unsettle me. No. He had removed it with such haste, there had to be something else in it, something he didn't want me to discover. But what? I needed to know. I got up as quietly as I could and put on my tracksuit. I was already wearing my socks as my feet were so cold in bed. I tied my hair back, then slid in a grip from my bedside table to keep my overgrown fringe out of the way. Slipping on my trainers, I kept watch that no one woke around me, then crept to the door and opened it, wincing at the enormous creek it let out. No one stirred so I was safe…for now.

I tiptoed down the corridor to the stairs but my rubber soles were conspicuously squeaky so I took them off and carried them. As a result, I slid precariously on the polished parquet floor, just narrowly missing a porcelain statue. I managed to get down the stairs in one piece and strode along the carpeted corridor to the white door of Mitchell's office. I carefully turned the ridged, copper knob…but it was locked. Why would he lock it, for goodness' sake? I removed the hair clip from my ponytail and prized it open so that it was like one long, straight piece of wire. Then I pushed it into the lock in an attempt to pick it. I'd seen it done in loads of films but I obviously wasn't doing it right as it wasn't working and it pinged back and onto the carpet in front of me.

"Give it here."

"Nyle? What are you doing here? And why are you dressed like a burglar?"

"What? I'm dressed all in black because I don't want to be seen. There…" he said, releasing the lock. "Anyway… why are you here…breaking into Mitchell's office?"

"I'm not breaking in…well, maybe just a little…"

"Shhhh. Someone's coming."

We dashed into the room and hid under Mitchell's desk. The night porter must've been checking up on things and shone a torch, illuminating the room, checking for unwanted guests like me and Nyle, I suppose, but he wasn't very thorough and left quite swiftly, locking the door behind him.

"Phew! That was close," I whispered. "At least you can pick the lock again to get us out. Where did you learn how to do that?"

"My dad's a locksmith."

"Oh." I nodded.

"You still haven't told me why you're here, Ellery."

"I want to get the ebonoid book that Mitchell took from me."

"Why?"

"There's something in it he doesn't want me to see…I'm sure of it."

"Then maybe you shouldn't see it."

"If ebonoidism…is that even a word?"

Nyle shrugged.

"If it runs in families, then maybe there's something about my father or his family in there. I mean, my mother's a Dweller so it's got to be on my father's side, right?"

"I suppose."

I pulled open the drawer and saw the book exactly where Mitchell had placed it. As I removed it, I saw his hag stone. I picked it up to examine it again. Something about it fascinated me. Mitchell had said that hag stones find *you*, not the other way around. Would this count as *finding me*? Perhaps not, in which case it might bring bad luck instead of good, so I reluctantly put it back. As I did, I noticed **THE BURGESS MANIFESTO** in bold black capital letters printed on a large, sealed envelope. The stone must have been resting on the words. I took it out but didn't open it. It was heavy, probably containing a number of documents. I knew I shouldn't have taken the envelope, but...I did. Somehow it was wrong to take the stone...but taking this was okay because I just wanted to read it. I wasn't going to keep it. It would be like borrowing it...sort of.

"What's that?"

"Just put it in your rucksack and let's go."

"What do you mean, *let's go*?"

"You're leaving, aren't you? You *were* running away?"

"Yes, but...I have to, Ellery. Nash will find me at school...I have to leave."

"That's why I'm coming with you."

"No, it's too dangerous."

"For who? You or me? I mean, if Nash gets wind of a juvenile ebonoid at school, I'm finished, aren't I? He'll kill me...no questions asked."

Nyle didn't answer.

"So where are we heading?" I asked.

"Erm…I don't know yet. I thought I'd just leave and see where it took me."

"Nyle…that's not a plan. It's a suicide mission straight to Nash, if you ask me. Have you got any money…any food and drink?"

He opened his rucksack to show me a small water bottle, an apple, a banana and a crumbled piece of donk.

"That's not enough," I said. "And what's *that*?"

"My ukulele."

"What do you need a ukulele for?"

"Music's important. It calms me down. Besides…my dad gave it to me for my thirteenth birthday. It's a thing among Magaecians…to hand down a musical instrument that's been in their family for generations when their child reaches the age of a decade and three. It'll bring us luck."

"It'll bring you a backache. Anyway…I've got an idea. We'll head back to my house in Tribourne…"

"But what about your mum?"

"She's staying with friends here in London…and she's taken the dog with her too. We can pick up some supplies and I've got some more money there we can use."

"All right. Come on…we should go before it gets light," whispered Nyle, holding up the straightened hair grip.

11

HUMANITY FOR THE MANIFESTO

We got on the night train and headed for Tribourne. There was a young couple snogging at the end of the carriage but they got off after three stops, leaving us alone in silence. Nyle went over his bag and took out the ebonoid book.

"Why do you suppose Mitchell didn't want you to have it?"

"Dunno," I replied, taking the book from him and reading aloud through the topics of each chapter. I couldn't find anything that seemed suspicious or clandestine and was a touch disappointed. "There's a chapter on misusing ebonoid energy...perhaps he thought I'd want to learn *the dark forces*," I growled sarcastically, waving my hands like an evil sorcerer. "There's *guidance for the juvenile*...erm...wait... *victims of dark ebonoid*...let's have a look at that chapter," I said, flicking to the page indicated in the contents.

"Hmmm…boring…boring…bla, bla, bla. It's all about people who have been killed by ebonoid hundreds of years ago," I said as I continued to plough through the tedious text. "Hang on…there's a bit here on the death of Darwin Burgess…and a photo of him with a group of people…"

"Pass it here," said Nyle, holding out his hand. "Yep… that's the old Magaecian Circle, I think," he started, pointing out the faces. "This man here, is Darwin Burgess…"

Darwin was dark-haired but fair-skinned with a look of sincerity in his blue, blue eyes. He appeared to have an athletic rugby-type build, someone who could probably handle himself in a crisis – although, after what happened to him – not well enough, it seemed. Besides…what can you tell from a photo anyway? I was never going to meet him so I guess I'd never know. As I scrutinised his face a bit more, it wasn't a face that I recognised and yet his expression was strangely familiar.

"There's Myerscough, of course…Knox and Kimberley Nibley-Soames," Nyle continued.

"Orford's parents?"

"Yeh…and that's Corliss Winterbourne. My mum grew up with her. Nash did terrible things to her and her family."

"Which one's Nash?"

Nyle put his finger on a man's face. "Him."

"He's beautiful…" I said, which was an odd thing to say about a man…a terrible man at that, whom I'd never met, but he was so striking…like an Adonis. He looked familiar but I couldn't place him. Besides, I'd never forget a face like that. I spotted a smiling young woman next to Nash and suddenly felt the blood drain from my cheeks. "What's *she* doing in the picture?" I blurted out indignantly.

"What do you mean?" Nyle laughed. "That's Nash's girlfriend…Nell Burgess, of course. No one knows what happened to her."

I held the book closer to my eyes in case I was mistaken… but how could I mistake a picture of my own mother. It might have been over a decade ago but it was Mum.

"You all right, Ellery? You're shaking."

I didn't answer.

"Ellery?"

"Yeh…I'm fine…just hungry. The next stop's ours," I said quietly as if in a trance and passed the book back to Nyle to put in his rucksack.

We got off the train and set off for the mile walk to the boring village of Tribourne. The pavement was barely visible as dawn was breaking. Birds chirped melodiously as sunlight slowly filtered through the sky and splashed the clouds with red.

"Ever heard the spell, *red sky in the morning, shepherd's warning*?" asked Nyle nonchalantly.

As I looked up, I could only imagine this was a terrible omen, and a horrible feeling inside my gut suggested my life was about to change.

"This is my house," I said, pointing to the tatty cottage across the road. "I've got the key."

It should have been comforting, being home again, but with the knowledge of Mum hiding out, in so much danger for all these years, it was unnerving instead. No wonder she was so protective of me. A terrible thought ran through my head. If Mum was Nash's girlfriend, would that make Nash my…? I didn't want to think about it.

"Help yourself to food if there is any," I said, sprinting up the stairs. "I'm dying for a wee!" When I got back to the kitchen, Nyle had buttered us some peanut butter on fresh bread and chopped some banana on top. I wondered why Mum had left the bread and fruit if she knew she was going to be away. She was always so over-the-top with stuff like that.

"Want a cup of tea?" I asked.

"Yes, please…no milk in mine."

"Why don't Magaecians drink milk?"

"Cow's milk?"

I nodded.

"It's pretty obvious, isn't it? I mean…why would you drink the breast milk of a cow? It's weird!"

"I guess…when you put it like that." I pondered for a moment then added, "Okay, if I'm going to fit in with Magaecian schoolkids, then I'm vegan too." I smiled, putting both hot cups of black tea on the table. I took a sip, which was a lot more palatable than I'd expected, then opened my hand across to Nyle. "Let's see it, then," I said.

"See what?" asked Nyle with a mouthful.

"The envelope…with the Burgess Manifesto."

"Mother Magae, Ellery! The *what*?" Nyle removed the envelope from his rucksack and examined it closely. "It's still sealed. You can't open it. It might be top secret or something. Mitchell will go spare."

"I highly doubt it. Burgess wanted to make sure everyone on the planet followed it, didn't he?"

Nyle passed it over anxiously, then couldn't stop himself from letting out the most enormous yawn. I must admit, I could've done with a bit of a nap too. Before I'd even started to break the envelope's seal, Nyle had nodded off, still sitting at the kitchen table. His head had fallen backwards so that he was snoring. He sounded like a walrus with a head cold. Perhaps it wouldn't hurt to have a few zzz's. I put my head on the table and nodded off too…

I don't know how long we'd been dozing when the sound of voices outside startled me.

"Someone's here," I whispered on hearing the front door creak. I grabbed the unsealed package and pushed Nyle awake before bundling him into the airing cupboard with me. We squashed into the sweaty cupboard like a pair of circus contortionists and held our breath. This proved to be quite difficult for Nyle as he'd stuffed his mouth with the leftover bread and peanut butter before squeezing in with me.

"She's not here," whispered a familiar voice.

"Thomas?" I said, opening the cupboard door to find not only Thomas but Letty as well.

"Happy Birthday!" they sang.

"How did you know we were here?" asked Nyle. "And where's Kemp? Chickened out?"

"Actually, it was Kemp's idea," said Letty, quick to defend him. "He found you by using the library tracker on your book, but his brother caught up with him and made him tell Myerscough."

"Myerscough?" shouted Nyle. "He'll kill us…I mean *really* kill us."

"He won't kill us," I said. "He will punish us, though." I suddenly got flashbacks of Lawson's Abattoir, which made me shudder. "How did you know I took the book back?"

"Mitchell came looking for you in the middle of the night. He was furious. He sent me, Kemp and Thomas to the library, where he grilled us about it. That's when Kemp thought about tracking your book...after Mitchell had stormed out looking for Myerscough."

"What are we going to do?" asked Thomas, eyeing up my bread and peanut butter, then placing my rucksack on the floor.

"Here," I said, passing him the bread. "You brought my rucksack?"

"Letty thought you might need a few things...girl toiletries and stuff," he said, turning up his nose.

"Thanks. I think what I'm going to need...is a Magaecian guru...someone to teach me enough to be able to reason with Nash."

"Reason with him? You can't reason with someone like Nash," said Nyle.

"But we must. That's what it's all about, isn't it? Finding a common ground, our similarities...rather than our differences. The solution lies with what will unite us – not what will divide us."

"Most gurus live in India or Tibet," said Nyle. "Mind you, my grandad said he knew a Sri Lankan guru who emigrated...to Wembley."

"Wembley?" I repeated. "Are you sure?"

"Yeah. I think he and his wife liked football."

We all started laughing.

"I don't suppose you know whereabouts in Wembley he lives?" I asked. "I mean, we can't just hang around Wembley Stadium hoping he comes along, can we?"

"Sure. Dave was Grandad's next-door neighbour. Not now, though – Grandad lives in a bungalow…bad hip."

"Dave? His name is Dave?"

"Dave Rupasinghe. Maybe he liked David Beckham…I don't know, do I?"

"What are we waiting for, then? We need to go to Wembley," I said, looking up train times on Nyle's mobile phone, which was charging up nicely in the kitchen socket.

"Why are we going, again?" asked Thomas.

"Because Nyle needs to run from Nash and…so do I."

"You? Why do *you* need to run?" questioned Thomas, licking his peanut-buttery fingers.

"Because if he finds out I'm an ebonoid, he'll kill me."

"What do you mean?"

"She means…" started Letty, "that *she's* the ebonoid, not Orford."

I looked across to Letty with a nod.

"Whoa! No way! I mean…right. I mean…don't worry," flapped Thomas. "We're fat friends, remember? We stick together, no matter what. Solid…and liquid…oily… greasy…"

"Yeh, okay. We get the picture," said Nyle.

"I think I need to learn how to channel my negative energy into a positive one so that I can do something good with it. I reckon Myerscough has plans to save us all through the Burgess Manifesto but he can't begin to implement it while Nash is killing everyone off."

"So where do you come in?" asked Letty.

"I'm not really sure. I have a feeling that being an ebonoid might be useful somehow."

"Not if you lose your temper, it won't be," added Nyle.

"That's the point, isn't it? I mean, I'm no match for Nash if I use negativity like he does...to hurt people. I'm never going to match the power he's acquired. I have a feeling it's all about positive energy. It overpowers negative. I just have to learn how to make it positive...and quick."

"First you'll need to get rid of that terrible temper of yours," said Nyle, grabbing his throat, pretending to throttle himself.

"Very funny, Nyle...very funny. Perhaps we should read the Burgess Manifesto. It's our duty...if we're going to save the world, right?" I smiled, not just outside but in. Changing the world was in my blood after all...in double, albeit conflicting, quantities.

I found some gooey chocolate brownies in the fridge and put them on the table for some extra energy while reading. It wasn't long before Letty got bored. She took out her pad to begin sketching. In fact, it wasn't long before my other friends lost interest too. It was quite a hefty wad of information to get through. I suppose it was now official...I was a nerd after all. I was used to reading loads and quite quickly too but I kept going until I got to the end. If I could summarise it in my head then I knew I could teach it to my friends.

"We don't have to do that marathon walk back to the station, do we?" groaned Thomas, wiping his sticky fingers all over his cream sweatpants, which was gross.

"It's only a mile, Thomas. Come on," I retorted as I put the Manifesto back into the envelope and into my rucksack. "We have a mission now."

"Do we?"

"Magaecians for the Manifesto!" screamed Letty, punching the air.

"You mean *humanity* for the Manifesto," I corrected.

"Humanity for the Manifesto!" repeated my friends as we piled our hands on top of one another.

"It might be best if we don't mention we've opened the Manifesto," I suggested. "Not yet…just in case."

My friends nodded. Before we set off for Wembley, I grabbed a few items and snacks, then locked the front door.

"Wait here a minute," I said quietly so as not to wake the village. "I'm popping the key through the Kings' letterbox next door. I'll only lose it if I keep it on me. Besides, Johnny King's parents are politicians so they must be trustworthy."

"My mum says you should never trust car salesmen, new hairdressers and most of all…politicians," said Letty.

"It's only to keep my key from getting lost. It's not like guarding the Crown Jewels or anything. Anyway…the Kings are only in Tribourne at weekends and school holidays. Their permanent address is in London. I won't be a minute."

I was back in a flash. Next stop: Dave.

12

IN SEARCH OF A GURU

Wembley was wet and windy. It was rush hour and the noisy road we walked along was in the middle of a chronic traffic jam. Horns were hooting and a few profanities escaped from car windows.

"That's the arch!" shouted Thomas, bouncing up and down, every part of his body needing to move as he pointed to Wembley Stadium's unmissable steel tiara. "I came here with Dad once...before he met Naomi. England versus Portugal. It was amazing inside...thousands and thousands of red seats all sheltered under that gigantic roof."

"I'm sure it was wonderful," said Letty kindly, "but we need to get going, don't we?"

Both Thomas and Nyle sighed, dropping their shoulders simultaneously as we continued on, following instructions from Nyle's phone, which led us to a small cul-de-sac called Beaulieu Gardens.

"That was Grandad's house, there on the end…so it must be this one," said Nyle, heading for the semi next door. As he rang the doorbell, we all stood pathetically behind him.

The door opened. An old woman dressed in a pink sari stood ramrod straight, smiling. It was an honest smile that made me feel safe. Her white hair was held up in an elegant bun to reveal her wrinkled but cultured face, dark skin and gentle brown eyes.

"Hello," she said quietly.

"We're looking for Mr Rupasinghe," said Nyle.

"Oh…I'm afraid you've missed him, child. He passed away over the summer."

My heart sank. I wasn't going to be able to get to India or Tibet for another guru. Mr Rupasinghe was my only reasonable hope.

"Perhaps I can help. I'm his wife, Daveena."

"Dave!" we all sang in unison.

"Yes, short for Daveena."

"I'm Nyle Pinkerton. My grandad used to live next door to you."

"Yes, indeed. We shared many a happy dinner with Clive and Janet." She smiled. "Come in. I've been expecting you. You must be…Letty, Thomas and…Ellery?" she said, extending handshakes.

We were spellbound. I reckon we were all thinking the same thing: that gurus must know everything.

"How did you know we were coming?" I asked.

"I told her," announced Myerscough, appearing from a room off the hallway.

Letty's cheeks turned white as she shook like a leaf and Thomas let out a little squeal.

"You need to get rid of that book if you don't want to be found," he said, holding out his hand for it.

I stood still, biting on my bottom lip, tasting a little blood as I struggled not to let on how disproportionately frightened I was of this man. I was also extremely angry with myself for not leaving the book behind. I knew it was linked to the Quinton House library so why was I so careless?

"I'll take the Manifesto as well," he growled.

I opened my rucksack and passed both items over.

"Why don't you come in, children?" said Dave calmly. "I've prepared a lovely breakfast for you."

"What a relief." Thomas sighed, his huge grin almost reaching his eyebrows.

"Not you, Brown," murmured Myerscough, blocking my way.

My heart sped up, causing me to gulp too much air into my lungs. My lips felt all tingly. Perhaps if I kept gulping, my lungs would inflate like a couple of balloons and I'd be able to fly away and avoid Myerscough's telling-off. I knew I was in big trouble, but he didn't know that I'd seen the photo of Mum in the ebonoid book. With any luck, this might work in my favour.

"You need to pay attention, my girl, and stop following your own agenda. I'm trying to help you here. Don't you understand? If you choose not to follow my advice—"

I could see his temper brewing and I was about to get the brunt of it if I didn't distract him quickly. "Sir," I butted in. "I'm sorry but...I think my mum's in danger."

139

"What?"

"My mum, she's in danger. I don't know how to warn her but I know that you know where she is. We need to warn her, Mr Myerscough…please, sir."

"And how would I know where she is?"

"Because you gave her the trackable library book from Quinton House… *Mealish Made Simple: Food spells for beginners.*"

"Very perceptive, Ellery. I don't suppose you earned that Saint Timothy's bursary for nothing, did you?" replied Myerscough with a shake of his head.

I pushed my index finger to my lips and mimed a *shush*, sending a fleeting glance in the direction of my friends, who were unaware of my nerdy scholarship.

Myerscough looked puzzled and mildly amused as he continued. "Your mother had many contacts with the old Magaecian Circle and also connections with Nash himself so she does need to be vigilant…but she's safe for now. You needn't concern yourself."

"Mr Myerscough…Mum said she'd tell me what I wanted to know about my dad and stuff when I'm home for Christmas…but…I kind of need to know a bit more now. I feel I ought to know as much as everyone else my age… about Nash and what he's done…and why Darwin Burgess was so great or not so great…"

"He *was* great and I won't have anyone say otherwise, do you hear me?"

"Yes, sir."

"We'll discuss it after breakfast but I must respect your mother's wishes if she wants to be the one to explain. She has her reasons, I'm sure."

I nodded and let out a disappointed sigh.

"Don't think you've got off lightly by changing the subject, young lady. I haven't finished that conversation yet."

Dave had made French toast, donk, and a savoury oat hash which was a bit like a curry porridge. I thought she'd made scrambled eggs but they turned out to be a spicy Indian tofu scramble, which was all delicious and very egg-like. We all tucked in with relish.

"Will you be able to help me, Dave…with my…*problem?*" I asked, sipping a cup of chocolate that was far too hot to swallow.

"It's a gift, Ellery…not a problem…unless you make it so. In answer to your question, *yes*, I can help you but not before you learn the basics. You need Mr Myerscough and indeed all your E.S.S. teachers long before my knowledge can really guide you."

I looked at the old lady who was a picture of serenity. "But you're…"

"I'm what?"

"Well…you're not exactly young, are you?"

"Ellery!" retorted Myerscough.

Dave started to giggle. "You think I might kick the bucket before I've taught you what you need to know?"

I thought it might be rude to answer her but it was exactly what I was thinking. She looked at least ninety.

"I'm not getting any younger…you're not wrong, Ellery, but my teachings will continue through my pupils… like Mr Myerscough here…and Mr Mitchell and his good wife, Laura. Yes…they were all students of mine, young apprentices who became great scholars and masters in their own right. They will all be able to help you, should I become one with Magae."

"I didn't mean…"

"It's okay, child. I know exactly what you meant." She smiled.

"So why didn't you help Nash?" I asked.

"I'm afraid Simeon didn't want to be helped."

"Simeon?"

"Yes, his parents were fond of Dweller names…which is why he changed it to Saxon, a more traditional Magaecian one. Pity, I thought it suited him."

"How did Burgess die?" I sneaked in artfully, hoping that if I directed my questions at the guru, she'd be more likely to answer honestly, unlike Myerscough.

"I'm not sure that's a question for Dave right now. Perhaps we could revisit that one later, Ellery," Myerscough butted in.

"Perhaps we could visit it now, Hendrick." Dave smiled in Myerscough's direction. "There's nothing to hide here… nothing. The truth is all she needs."

Myerscough shifted uneasily in his seat. He swiped his large fingers back and forth across his furrowed brow, then did the same over his stubbly chin as if limbering up his face before letting out his story. He cleared his throat before reluctantly beginning.

"Darwin Burgess was ambushed."

"By Nash and his men?"

The anguish on Myerscough's face gave my insides an uncomfortable feeling but I didn't dare show it in case he used it as an excuse to stop.

"No…by Dwellers."

"Dwellers? But I thought—"

"Are you going to interrupt me after every sentence, Ellery?"

"No, sir."

Myerscough let out a puff. "It was that period between Christmas and New Year. Darwin and Nell's parents were over from Ireland and Darwin asked me to pop by to say hello. I hadn't seen his folks in ages. I adored Brendan and Shauna Burgess. I'd known them almost as long as I'd known Darwin…probably since my early twenties. They were like a second set of parents to me. I offered to drive them back to their hotel in London but Darwin insisted I stay to spend some time with Nell. He said he had a meeting in Whitehall so it would work out well for him. I'd hardly seen Nell since she and Nash had become an *item* so the thought of catching up with her was an appealing one. Women were always bewitched by Nash. He was charming, handsome – a slick, slimy demon, and Nell was infatuated with him." Myerscough's lips were tight as he spat out the last words. "We were chatting…having quite a laugh actually. I'd forgotten how funny she could be, when the phone rang. She waltzed into the kitchen, leaving me to snigger into my coffee. It had been such a warm, cosy atmosphere, and then it turned just like that. I heard crockery smashing – like the sound of gunshots. I ran into the kitchen to find Nell bent over. She was hysterical. She said she'd killed her family. She said it was all her fault. I couldn't make sense of anything she was saying."

"Did you make her a hot chocolate, sir?" asked Thomas.

"I gave her a brandy, which seemed to calm her enough to form a sentence or two. She choked out the shocking news she'd just received on the phone. The death of Darwin and both her parents…in a car accident. She was inconsolable. She said it was her fault…that she'd told Nash exactly where her brother was heading…details of the meeting… what time it was to be held and where exactly it was taking place."

"She set him up," I announced, forgetting I'd agreed to keep my mouth shut until Myerscough had finished his story. "She led him into a trap," I continued, raising my voice and clenching my fists. "But why? Why did she do that? How could she do that to her own flesh and blood?" I was seething. Why did I have the worst parents in the universe? Why did fate hand me this DNA that would mean I had no chance in life of becoming anything but foul, corrupt and evil? It was so unfair. Maybe my only sensible option was to head straight for Nash to kill me – just get it over with before I did anything unforgivable.

Myerscough grabbed my wrists so hard that it hurt as he slapped my hands together in the namaste position. His angry eyes burned into my soul, filling me with a sudden guilt and disgust at my response, which had been such an inappropriately selfish one. Did that make me bad already?

"No," he growled. "She didn't set him up. Nell would never do that to her brother."

If there was such a thing as a guilt-saturation point, then I'd reached it. I'd hastily come to the wrong conclusion about my own mother. I was officially on that road to being bad… worse than bad…despicable even.

"She'd apparently spoken to Darwin months ago about her relationship with Nash and how volatile it had become. She'd been naive. She thought Nash might join forces with Darwin and together they'd put things right with Magae. But he was becoming more and more irrational, dishonest and cruel, and Nell was frightened. Nash could be cunningly persuasive and she'd already told him more than she wanted. Darwin was concerned at the danger she might be in if she stayed with him. Nell was all too aware that if she left Nash, he would most likely kill her but if she remained, she'd be forced to give up information which would leave Darwin vulnerable – a sitting duck."

"So what did they do?" asked Letty.

"Nell said that Darwin, being *Darwin*, decided he could use the situation to his advantage. He told Nell to make sure Nash knew exactly where he and his Manifesto would be. Each time Nash sent a couple of henchmen to intercept the Manifesto, Darwin would give it to them page by page with a full explanation as to why Nash must compromise. He said it wasn't the end to Magae's problems, but it was the beginning to the solution."

"I don't understand," said Letty. "Why didn't they just kill him?"

"Because Magaecians are taught from a very early age to *listen* before they act and to *pause* before they react. Using this Magaecian trait would give Darwin an edge. He would deliver the most convincing spells, influencing Nash's men to reconsider their point of view. Darwin was a brilliant man and it worked. As more and more men were sent…so more and more men changed their minds in Darwin's favour. Of course, those men that returned to Nash with this new idea were never seen again. Those that didn't return to Nash went into hiding for obvious reasons. With so many of Nash's men changing sides, Darwin knew it was only a matter of time before Nash stopped sending his people to instead come himself. So Darwin gave the Manifesto to Nell…to give to me…that day. He wasn't sure Nash still had the capacity to listen and he was realistic in the possibility that he might not return after they met."

"I still don't understand," said Letty.

"Nell told Nash that Darwin's biggest fear was agribusiness."

"You mean farming?" I asked.

Myerscough nodded. "Darwin was bound to be threatened by farmers if he was too radical in how he intended to change things. Dwellers needed to cut down on their meat consumption if they were to have any chance of addressing climate change and greenhouse gas emissions. Darwin had to get this point across, but he wasn't stupid. He knew that this would have a devastating effect on the livestock industry, which is why he created the Burgess Manifesto. He'd worked out a way for Dwellers to continue to eat meat—"

"Just less of it – which would reduce gas emissions…I'm guessing, of course," I added quickly, not wanting to alert Myerscough to the fact that I'd read the Manifesto.

"Yes…spot on, Ellery, but eating another's flesh goes against all Magaecian beliefs. We believe the only way to find your inner peace – Magaecians call it 'neth gilne' – is to live a non-violent life. That means not killing animals as well as not killing people."

146

"I don't suppose Nash will ever find his geth nil... What was it again?" asked Thomas.

"Neth gilne," sniggered Nyle.

"Yeah...well, he won't find...*that*."

"Is that why Nash hated Darwin so much?" I asked.

Myerscough didn't answer, which produced an uncomfortable silence in the room.

"So what happened, sir?" asked Letty.

"Nash told the people at the top...in the meat industry... the ones that had the most to lose...the ones that could lose millions and millions in cash, that Darwin was going to Parliament to implement the cutting out of all meat in order to save the planet."

"But that's not true!" I shouted.

"Exactly...but they didn't know that. Unfortunately, where huge amounts of money are concerned, corruption and dark deeds often follow...and...on that fateful day... when Darwin expected Nash to confront him, Darwin's car was forced off the road and into a ditch where it mysteriously caught fire." Myerscough pretended to scratch at his nose so that we wouldn't notice him flicking away his tears. "Nash hadn't sent any more of his followers..."

"He sent Dwellers instead, didn't he? Dwellers that didn't listen to spells," added Nyle.

"What about Nell?" I asked, curious to know how my mum managed to escape.

"If the Manifesto wasn't found with Darwin, Nash would very soon conclude that Nell must have it and he wasn't going to rest until it was in his possession."

"Poor Nell," whispered Letty.

"Anyone that had read it or had a connection with it was going to be in danger from Nash, which is why so many people on the Circle went into hiding."

"But what about you, sir?" I asked. "You knew what was in it."

"Yes, I did, but...Nash and I grew up together and..." He paused. "Well, we had an unwritten rule. Our families were close, and you don't harm family..."

That was a pretty weird remark. If there was one thing Myerscough wasn't, it was lame...and that answer was totally lame. I couldn't challenge him, not after everything he'd told us, but he was definitely hiding something, something I'd have to figure out for myself.

"It's a shame poor Darwin didn't get a chance to share his Manifesto," began Dave philosophically. "Darwin was very gifted not just at getting his point across but also at listening. For Darwin Burgess, violence was never an option even when dealing with Nash. He would go out of his way to hear both sides of every story, always open-minded. His intention was always to listen to why people were enraged, then find a solution to deal with the cause of their anger rather than the anger itself. Fighting anger with more anger solves nothing. It stokes the fire of hatred instead of putting it out."

"But Nash knows she's alive...Nell, I mean. He knows, doesn't he?"

Myerscough threw me a grave look, then nodded.

We all sat in silence. It was a horrifying story and an even more dreadful burden for Mum to bear. Nash had killed the whole Burgess family and now he was coming for her. I suspect he knew nothing of me, which is why Mum changed her name. I didn't really understand where I fitted into all of this but maybe it was going to be up to me to finish what my Uncle Win...Uncle *Dar*win had started.

"No one can solve this alone," said Dave. "We must trust each other and look for the courage to be positive. We, as teachers, will respect you and never expect you to partake in anything we wouldn't do ourselves, and you, as children, should respect your teachers and do the same. Treat everyone with dignity whether they be Magaecian or Dweller. If you believe yourself better or more powerful than everyone else, this can only lead to violence and hatred until you no longer see how closely related we all are. Always keep in mind what we ultimately want as human beings...to remain and live together on Magae. This is what all humanity craves. It is our common denominator."

These were wise and reassuring words and yet I couldn't breathe as they choked me. I nodded, pretending not to be afraid but adrenaline pumped through me as though someone had left an adrenaline tap on, causing my whole body to shake.

"Let's do a little totem exercise, shall we?" suggested Dave, putting her hands together and lightening the mood. "Have you got your totem stones with you?"

"They'll be making them this term, Dave," said Myerscough.

"I see. Well...you can pick a stone now, if you like... even if it's only temporary. I've loads in my back garden. You can learn how to decorate them another time...when you're at school with your teachers." She led us through French

149

patio doors and into her small garden, the lawn of which was covered in a shimmering gold autumnal blanket. The leaves danced with a delicate elegance as the breeze blew across them. "Just pick a stone that takes your attention… then bring it inside with you."

After a while, she walked over to Thomas, who was clearly finding it difficult to make up his mind as he stood still, holding an enormous boulder.

"Thomas, child," began Dave, calmly picking up some alternatives for him. "Magaecians like to keep their totem stones on their person…in their pockets usually…or they may even make them into an item of jewellery."

"You're going to encounter serious problems with that one, Sticky," said Myerscough. "Unless your mother gets you a pair of trousers with monumental pockets."

Thomas put the large rock down in favour of a small, purplish oval stone; Letty had an odd-shaped rusty-coloured one and Nyle's was a grey one which had splintered to reveal a caramel-looking inside. Myerscough gestured to me to show the one I'd picked. I opened my hand.

"You've picked a *black* stone," he growled, then threw a look of concern in Dave's line of vision.

"A stone, no matter what the colour, dark or light, is a natural element made up of Magae's minerals. Having it in your possession will connect you to Magae and this in turn, will help connect you to your totem animal." She smiled at me and then at Myerscough, which seemed to shut him up.

"Okay, everyone…bring your stones and follow me," said Dave, walking us through to a cosy living room area where there was an unlit fireplace. "Now, take a cushion and come sit on the floor with me. You too, Hendrick."

We got ourselves comfortable on the floor then waited for her instruction.

"Hold your stone between both palms and close your eyes. Just relax and let your imagination guide you but not mislead you. Take deep breaths…good…we'll begin. You need to enter a chamber in your mind. It can be a cave, a tree…a catacomb if you're into creepy stuff…just some sort of hideaway where you feel safe. As you walk through it, you'll come to an exit onto a grassy field, luscious, fragrant and green. Let Magae fill you with peacefulness so that your totem may enter your setting. Feel its power, how it moves. Does it make a sound? Check out its form, its colour… perhaps you can hear what it's thinking. Some totems will tell you why they have chosen you and how they may help you… but for now just enjoy its company. Thank it for presenting itself and ask for some sort of proof that will confirm truth in your totem choice. It might perhaps present itself in a dream…in markings in a tree or a pattern on a cushion… even a resemblance of its shape on a piece of toast. Or you might come across it in a picture or on TV. I want you now to slowly move back to your hideaway and feel safe and relaxed. Take deep breaths…about three should do it until you feel connected to Margae…alive and perceptive, then you can leave your chamber and come back into my living room, opening your eyes slowly…"

We all opened our eyes and looked at Dave for an explanation. I, for one, was really confused.

"You can share your experience or maybe you're still not

sure what your totem is and wish to keep it to yourself for now. What about you, Thomas?"

Thomas shook his head. "I think I'll wait for a while, thanks."

I waited for him to give his reasons why but he didn't, choosing instead to look at his shoes, which had collected a couple of wet leaves on the soles.

"Okay. Would you like to share anything, Letty?"

"Yes, please. My totem is a heron. I felt its broad wings become part of my energy, its freedom to soar and glide. It was amazing! Its long legs were my legs and I could suddenly see more acutely."

"That's marvellous, Letty," said Dave. "Those guided by the heron totem usually stand out by their gentleness. They have a unique, creative quality which allows them to project their Magaec on those around them." Dave handed Letty a book on heron totems from a rickety bookshelf next to the fireplace.

"You look a little disturbed, Ellery. The exercise was meant to relax you, child."

"I'm confused, Dave. I thought my totem was an elephant. When I came out of my cave…there it was, standing tall… intelligent, focused, powerful and strong…but…"

"But what?" asked the guru.

"But then another animal appeared and stood in front of the elephant."

"What animal?"

"It was a badger. Not just any badger, but a honey badger. I have a bookmark that has a picture of one so I know it's not your common or garden one. The thing is…when I felt the energy of my totem, it wasn't the elephant that I felt, but the honey badger."

"That's because the honey badger is your true totem. The elephant is there to protect you, and you need to keep it in your picture. That elephant will remain loyal until the end."

"Honey badger," growled Myerscough. "I might've known. They're famous for not backing down to anyone and don't like being told what to do. It's definitely your totem. I should have seen it…so obvious. Nothing but trouble."

"Interesting," said Dave, narrowing her eyes. "Beware, Ellery. Honey badgers have a dark side and must learn to control their emotions."

"And their temper," Nyle butted in.

"Hmmm. Achieving balance can prove difficult and you must work constantly to keep a positive energy within you. Your totem is easily turned by those with similar power or wisdom or a standing that can rival your own. Use your positive traits at all times. Your totem possesses a wisdom to comprehend human nature which can bring great compassion. You have an extremely dynamic totem, Ellery, capable of harnessing great power. Use it wisely…or it might well destroy you."

It was a lot to take in and Dave looked concerned…as did Myerscough, who was fidgeting with his stubbly chin. I didn't know what to think. I had goosebumps, not from unease or trepidation but because I believed I might actually have the world's most fearless animal as my totem. I could take on any enemy no matter their size or strength. Could this qualify as being *totally Hawk*? I fiddled with my mouth, attempting to appear contemplative but mostly to hide the smirk from my delight.

"Okay, younglings," said Myerscough, standing up. "It's time we were making tracks."

Nyle's complexion paled.

"Listen up, please, boys and girls. You are all far safer at school than you are traipsing round the countryside on your own where you're a lot more vulnerable to Nash and his people. You are all protected by the M…U…S…I…C."

"That spells music." Thomas laughed.

"It stands for the Magaecian Union for the Safety of Innocent Children. Mrs Huckabee has gone to great lengths to ensure that this protection remains in place for your security. It applies to all students at any E.S.S. not just Quinton."

"So – what about Aiken Thorne?" I asked. "He was still at school."

"Indeed," replied Myerscough. "Unfortunately the protection lasts only until a youngling reaches the age of sixteen. Aiken is almost eighteen so no longer covered. However, this isn't about sixth-formers, it's about you lot. You're safer at school. Am I understood?"

"Yes, sir," we all chanted.

"No more bright ideas about running off, please. Any concerns – you talk to me or any other member of staff, for that matter." Myerscough's eyes focused on us individually to make sure we were all intimidated enough to think twice about disobeying.

"Ellery, child," Dave whispered, breaking the anxious silence. "I have a couple of exercises you can try to redirect your negativity should you need to. Come with me."

I followed her back to the kitchen, where she started packing up treats, hopefully for us to take on our way.

"When anger approaches and control is resistant, hold your anger and reverse it...on yourself. In other words, let it hit you. It can't injure the producer...although, I imagine it can cause discomfort...something you might well have to learn to endure. If you acknowledge this pain as something in your control, you may be able to neutralise it by thinking positive. Don't fight hatred with more hatred. Find a way to make things neutral. Source the anger, find the root of its cause, then detach yourself. Nash dishes out pain to others because he is nothing more than a bully. This is not power but weakness and insecurity. You must rise above this way of thinking. Refrain from playing his game and you will have true strength. You need to be an intelligent ebonoid so that when anger strikes, you exhibit calmness. Let your anger become a motivation to channel your energy into positive results. You have the capacity within you at all times to seek a solution. It isn't necessary to prove yourself right or someone else wrong. There is always a common bond that links enemy with ally. Find the bond of similarity and eliminate the differences."

My chest tightened, taking my heart into custody before it had a chance to escape. What if I couldn't do any of those things Dave advised? What if I turned out like my father? My head was spinning.

"Ellery," said Dave, taking my hands gently in hers. "You have the potential to do extraordinary things with your life. You may not realise it now, but being an ebonoid is a wonderful gift if you use it correctly and veraciously. I wish you only good fortune on your journey, child." She removed her hands, then smiled as she placed them together, gesturing namaste, which I returned.

"Oh…and one more thing," she added, while carefully wrapping some home-made chocolate. "Happy Birthday." She placed the chocolate into a little green box, adding a matching green ribbon on the top before handing it to me. "Hendrick told me."

"Thanks, Dave," I said.

Dave and I walked to the front door where the others were waiting. She passed Myerscough a selection of snacks to put in his large rucksack.

"We'd better step on it if we're to catch up with the rest of Year 8 before tonight," said Myerscough.

As we marched out through Dave's front door and onto Wembley's Beaulieu Gardens once more, Myerscough held me back.

"Happy Birthday, by the way," he barked at me.

13

HAPPY HONEY

We followed Myerscough into the next road where he'd parked his jeep. As the wind blew across my face with an uncomfortable chill, I only hoped he wasn't going to leave his window down again.

"Here…you navigate, please, Ellery," said Myerscough, slapping me with a yellowing, tatty old map. I half expected to find an X to mark the spot of hidden treasure, it was such an ancient papyrus.

"Haven't you got satnav?" I asked.

"Where we're going, satnav doesn't reach."

Letty, Nyle and Thomas piled into the back of the jeep while I strapped myself in the front next to Myerscough…

"Ellery!"

I opened my eyes to a large man's angry face. I'm not sure how long he'd been calling my name but I was a goner after the first five minutes of the journey.

"No point asking what you saw on the way."

"Sorry, sir. I think I might have nodded off."

"*Might have?* Hmmmm."

Myerscough parked next to two other jeeps in an open village car park. He got out and unlocked the small storage trunk to retrieve his enormous rucksack which, once hoisted onto his back, seemed less enormous.

"Follow me," he commanded, massaging and manipulating his shoulder like he had rheumatism or something. Mum used to do it all the time with her foot. She fell off a horse and broke her ankle when she was a kid and said it always ached when it was going to rain.

Letty closed her sketch pad, which was probably full of scenes and important landmarks from the journey. She flashed a page at me, showing a caricature of Myerscough with an enormous frown and a gigantic square chin. I let a giggle slip, alerting Myerscough to look my way. We followed our teacher, passing a village green not unlike the one in Tribourne, then continued along a road past a couple of old cottages.

"Here," he said, throwing over some sort of snack that I couldn't identify, unlike Nyle who popped it in his mouth straight away with a pleased smile.

"It's halva. You know? Sesame seeds and syrup made into a slab. Delicious…and good for your bones…lots of calcium. It'll give you some energy. It's quite a long walk, I'm afraid."

Thomas spluttered as he shoved the whole thing in his mouth. I cautiously bit off just a little piece, which was lovely and sweet but had a peculiar texture…like cement; not that I'd ever eaten cement.

"Do all Magaecians eat this?" I asked.

"I don't know," replied Myerscough. "I bought it from your local Tribourne grocery store. I expect Chef MacBrennan could rustle up something similar. That woman's got a food spell for almost everything."

We reached a muddy track that continued forever, surrounded by a patchwork quilt of green and gold fields. Magae's fresh, earthy fragrance calmed me as I sucked in the air.

"This way," said Myerscough, taking us down a narrow path, which headed into a wood of twisted trees. The muted sun fell on the few leaves still clinging to summer's memory despite the arrival of autumn weeks ago. A whispering breeze judged us as we trespassed with little regard, trampling over leafy dead relatives. We reached a clearing but the sun had been held hostage by some savage clouds that turned the sky a dark steely grey.

"Did anyone notice a red sky this morning?" asked Myerscough, looking back from the front as we followed in pairs – me with Letty while Nyle walked with Thomas at the back.

"Yes, sir," answered Nyle, loudly. "Ellery and I spotted one."

"Anyone know what it means?"

"It's an indicator of rain coming," answered Nyle.

"Yes, it is. The wind is blowing from the east, bringing unsettled, possibly stormy weather. Take a deep breath and smell your surroundings. Smells are often more conspicuous before rain comes, especially the smell of vegetation. Plants and flowers sense when rain is imminent so that

159

they can readily open up to receive water. Always observe the vegetation around you to give you the information you need," he said, turning to us again. "Then there's the clouds, of course," he continued. "Remember that rain falls from low clouds. So, the higher the clouds, the better the weather. If there are low, dark clouds and the wind's blowing from the east, the pressure will be dropping and rain's inevitable. The more weather signs you can interpret, the more accurate you can be with your decisions for your route and your safety."

We continued for ages, passing field after field after field. The breeze was picking up, howling eerie chords in the gloomy sky. A cluster of gunshots came our way, scaring a group of birds which rocketed from a large tree, peppering the sky like a sooty chimney.

"Is that to stop them from eating the crops in the fields, sir?" asked Letty.

"That's not aimed at the birds. Now get running…to that tree over there," answered Myerscough with a disturbing urgency. "Run in a zigzag. It's harder to hit a vital organ so injury's less severe."

All four of us stood still like a group of idiots.

"Now!" he screamed, bolting us into zigzaggy action. "Where's Sticky?"

Thomas had tripped over, landing headfirst into a wide, boggy puddle.

"Get up!" yelled Myerscough. "Get up!"

But Thomas remained face down. He was frozen in fear, grabbing handfuls of mud for comfort but getting none as his body sank deeper and deeper into the mud. Myerscough sprinted in a straight line and grabbed Thomas by his coat collar before hoisting him, throwing him like a sack of potatoes, onto his back. The large man let out a grimacing cry as he headed back to join us under the tree. He held one arm across his body to keep Thomas in place, while the other hung lifelessly by his side. He knelt down to let Thomas off, then grabbed at his shoulder.

"What's wrong, sir?" I asked.

"It's dislocated. An old injury which comes back to haunt me more often than is bloody convenient," he replied as he gripped his shoulder with a squeeze.

I didn't ask how he'd originally come by the injury as I suspect it might've been from a session of torture years ago, courtesy of Nash and his mates.

"Why is Nash trying to kill us?" I asked.

"They're not Magaecians shooting, Ellery...they're Dwellers."

"Dwellers?"

"They don't like our kind," said Myerscough, struggling with his rucksack. "We can't stay under this tree, there's a storm coming," he continued, gritting his teeth. "Open it, will you, please, Ellery?" he asked, passing me his rucksack.

"Yes, sir. Of course."

"There should be a small bottle of honey in there...a red bottle."

"I thought Magaecians didn't eat honey," I said as I rummaged through to find a small black bottle...

"I said *red*!"

I came across the red bottle, the size of a small jar of Marmite, labelled *HAPPY HONEY: Magae's Miracle.*

"It's medicinal...now hand it over."

Myerscough ripped the lid off with his teeth then took a large, sticky swig before passing it back to me. Taking a deep breath, he lifted his dislocated shoulder with the other hand to the back of his head and did some sort of manoeuvre to produce an almighty crack. He bellowed out an anguished cry, followed by a loud sigh of relief.

"That's better," he said. He stood up...then thumped immediately down face first, unconscious.

"Mr Myerscough...sir?" I said, trying to shake him awake.

"We're all going to die!" wailed Thomas.

"No, we're not," snapped Nyle. "They've stopped shooting for the moment, anyway. Perhaps they've given up."

"Or maybe they're reloading." Letty covered her mouth, instantly realising that she shouldn't have said that.

I tried to quickly change the subject. "What kind of honey is this?" I asked, shoving my finger into the bottle to try some. "It's not very sweet for honey."

"Let's have a taste," chirped Thomas, finger at the ready to dip into the treacly bottle. "Not bad, I suppose," he said, licking his lips before passing it to Letty who did the same.

"Give it here," demanded Nyle with an outstretched hand. "Yuck! That smells disgusting," he said, creasing up his face as he examined the writing on the bottle. "Wait a minute. This is *silly sugar*."

"Silly sugar?" said Letty, giggling.

"Yeh...made by Nepalese bees, the biggest bees on Magae. They pollinate psychedelic flowers to produce *Happy Honey*. It's meant to make you happy. Magaecians use it as a painkiller. It dulls the pain by spacing you out."

"You mean intocshic…ashhhionnn…" slurred Thomas with a chortle.

"You're all as good as smashed." Nyle laughed, flipping up his hood as the rain was getting heavier.

Letty started giggling at Thomas, which set me off too. Thunder crashed through the air, followed by a sky-splitting streak of lightning a couple of minutes later, but all we could do was to stagger around sniggering like a group of old drunks.

"If lightning's less than sixty seconds after thunder, it means the lightning's very close," said Nyle in a more serious tone. "We need to get out of here."

Letty, Thomas and I nodded in agreement before breaking down in belly laughs.

"It's not funny!" yelled Nyle. "How are we going to move *him*?" He turned his face to the inanimate Myerscough.

Thomas and I were shaking our heads, donning enormous grins while Letty amused herself by making raspberry noises. My head felt completely disassociated from my body. As I looked at my hands, they didn't appear to belong to me. Another permeating blast of thunder and yet we weren't frightened, too busy cracking up with our psychedelic situation. The lightning took less than a minute to follow, which meant that we were sheltering in the most dangerous place, under a tree.

"You girls take his feet and we'll take his arms," ordered Nyle, who was the only one of us making any sense.

It was hopeless. We couldn't coordinate our limbs and kept laughing and sniggering. Nyle sat Myerscough up like a living corpse then put his head under one of his muscular arms, which probably weighed more than Nyle's whole body. "Please help me…*please*."

I took the arm with Nyle, leaving Thomas and Letty to lift the other one. We managed to get him up – still laughing of course – and moved away from the trees, dragging Myerscough's heavy feet behind to dig out two parallel muddy channels, which quickly filled with rainwater as the storm progressed. We were now in an open space which made us vulnerable – not only from the shooting Dwellers, who incidentally seemed to have given up shooting now that it was pouring with rain…but also from being hit by lightning. Thomas fell over his unsteady feet, setting Letty off into raptures of laughter. This resulted in Myerscough's full weight shifting onto me and Nyle with the predictable outcome of falling on each other – me onto Nyle and Myerscough onto both of us. I should have been terrified of suffocating but instead I found the situation mysteriously comical…unlike Nyle of course, who managed to slide himself out from under the pile-up, pulling me out with him.

"We need to crouch," said Nyle. "Squat down and try to be as small as possible…and put your head between your knees. We probably should spread out so that we don't all get hit together, but I think, given you're all plastered, maybe not." He tried to curl Myerscough up into a ball on the grass but the man was a giant unconscious dead weight.

We crouched like four human balls on the slippery grass, waiting to be electrocuted, if we weren't pelted to death first by the gruelling rain hitting at our bodies with such ferocity. My surroundings blended into one green blob. I think Nyle was holding his breath so I held mine too. At the muzzy realisation that we might all be killed, I decided to let go of my breath and lighten the mood.

"How about we divulge our darkest secret," I said, spitting through the rain as it washed over my skin. I felt a little more in control of my lips and what was coming out from them. I suspect the effects of the *Happy Honey* were slowly wearing off. "You first, Letty."

Letty giggled as she remained curled up with her head between her knees. "Okay," she began. "I'll tell. I've got a massive crush on Mr Mitchell."

"Everyone's got a crush on Mr Mitchell." Nyle laughed. "That man's seriously cool."

"Totally Hawk?" I asked.

"I guess."

"What about a secret from you then, Thomas?" I asked.

"You've got to promise not to tell," he snorted.

"We promise, don't we?"

"We promise," chorused Nyle and Letty.

"My totem's a pig. I mean, can you imagine the fun Orford Nibley-Soames would have with that?"

"Pigs are really cool, Thomas," said Letty. "In the totem drawings book I got from the Quinton library, it said they're resistant to snake venom because of the thickness of their skin."

"So? It's not like I'm going to find a snake any time soon, is it?"

"That depends," replied Letty. "Apparently…Nash's totem is a snake, you know?"

Thomas went silent. I wasn't sure if he was pleased with this new information or whether he'd just nodded off in his state of stupor.

"What about you, Nyle?" I enquired.

"Me? I don't have any dark secrets."

"Everyone's got at least one secret," slurred Thomas.

"Besides," I added, "we might all be hit by lightning in a minute. You wouldn't want to die not having shared your secret with anyone, would you?"

Nyle said nothing.

"Nyle?"

"Okay…but you might not want to remain friends after I've told you."

"We'll chance it," screamed Thomas over a loud crash of thunder. "We're fat friends, aren't we?"

"All right…seeing's we might be burned to a crisp at any moment. Orford Nibley-Soames…is my first cousin on my mum's side. My dad's mum was a Dweller, then became a Magaecian when she got married. The Nibley-Soameses never accepted my dad's family as Magaecians so when my mum, a Nibley-Soames, married my dad, they never spoke to her again."

"Their loss," said Letty.

As the lightning grew nearer, I closed my eyes tightly to shut it out.

"You haven't told us yours, Ellery," said Nyle, his voice tense and shaky.

"Mine's the darkest secret of all. If it were a competition, I'd win hands down."

"What could be worse than having Orford as your cousin?" shouted Nyle over another explosive thunderclap.

"Having Saxon Nash as your father!" I screamed.

"What did you say?"

166

I removed my head from between my knees to see my friends sitting bolt upright, stunned into sober silence.

"That's why Mitchell didn't want me having the ebonoid book. It had a picture of Nash's girlfriend, which I instantly recognised as my mum."

"So your mum's Nell Burgess?" stuttered Nyle.

I nodded. "Still want me as your friend, Nyle?"

"But that means Darwin Burgess was your uncle… making you, my fat friend, totally Hawk!"

I'd seen only the worst possible scenario to be related to Nash instead of the best possible scenario being related to Burgess. Not only that, but Nyle thought I was totally Hawk. I smiled and mouthed *thank you* to my fat friend.

"What's going on?" croaked Myerscough, gingerly getting to his feet. "I always underestimate the power of that honey."

"You did have quite a lot, sir," I said.

"The storm's passing. Come on, younglings, it's not too much further…thirty minutes tops."

I was expecting to hear a groan from Thomas but I think he was eager to get moving, however long it took. We all were.

We eventually reached a building clad in natural wood strips, like an oversized rustic cabin. Blending into the background, it was overshadowed by a regiment of tall trees that stood to attention guarding their territory with pride. It was a sight for sore eyes, screaming warmth and comfort and most of all, safety.

"We were worried," said Mr Mitchell, running towards us.

I couldn't help but look in Letty's direction, who had turned a shade of beetroot.

"I dislocated my shoulder and passed out," said Myerscough, failing to mention the *Happy Honey*. "These younglings behaved with great maturity and should be highly commended with an appropriate number of points on their rainbows."

We grinned at each other as Myerscough was whisked away by the teachers for some medical attention. I wondered if the outcome would have been the same were it not for Nyle being the only one in control of his senses.

"Hot chocolate?" asked Dr Ramsay.

I was relieved to see she hadn't been fired after all.

"Yes, please," I answered with the others.

"Okay," she continued efficiently. "So that's one for Mr Marks, one for Miss Brown, one for Mr Pinkerton and one for Miss...Letty."

"My first name's Letty, Miss."

"Right. One more hot chocolate for Miss Letty Letty. Dwellers do have unusual names."

Letty rolled her eyes with a smile but didn't contradict Dr Ramsay. If she felt anything like I did, the last thing she'd have wanted was to go into a lengthy explanation about her surname. I was feeling awful, achy all over and a pounding headache into the bargain. I imagined it might be how you'd feel if you had a hangover. Kemp came up and hugged us all, even me, which was unexpected. He took Letty's hand and walked her, dripping wet, to the kitchen for hot chocolate. We followed, the young weary travellers, sodden, but oh, so thankful to be alive.

"Happy Birthday!" screamed my classmates in the kitchen, surrounding a large birthday cake alight with thirteen candles.

"Here," barked Myerscough, slipping me a badly wrapped present. "It was your father's. It's been in your family for generations."

I unwrapped it to find a wooden flute. It was quite beautiful and had an oddly comforting smell of almond oil and old wood that had been well preserved through time. As I examined it further I found tiny animal carvings on the side of it.

"Totems through the ages," added Myerscough. "Through family generations."

There was an otter at the bottom, above that a wolf, then an owl and finally an elephant.

"Thank you, sir."

I was excited at the prospect of learning to play it until I caught Mitchell's unyielding gaze. Those well-earned rainbow points might soon be taken away for breaking and entering his office and worse still, stealing from his desk drawer. I took a deep breath. It was my birthday after all. I decided to enjoy the moment while I could and worry about Mitchell later.

14

THE BURGESS MANIFESTO

We spent the rest of the term at the cabin with Myerscough, Ademola and Hayhurst as our permanent tutors interspersed with visiting teachers who must've taken it in turns to travel around the countryside teaching the rest of the school in various areas. Mr Mitchell took it upon himself to give me extra lessons, working off my punishment for breaking into his office and stealing... although I saw it more as *borrowing*. His aim was to get me to wholly connect with and become my totem. This would help me to redirect my temper and adjoin with Magae's rhythm like my Magaecian ancestors before me. I had also worked hard in Mealish and was proud to say that I could produce a decent donk thanks to Chef MacBrennan. I had a new wealth of knowledge on harmful and helpful plants and spices to eat, as well as how to know if a plant was poisonous or edible.

Mr Ademola taught us Magaecian folklore and myths, which was one of my favourite lessons. It quickly became clear to me that Magaecian women were far more valued in society than Dweller women. There were many female Magaecian warriors through time commanding great respect, following their own minds as women in balance and in harmony with men as equals, rather than in competition. It was accepted among all Magaecians that men and women were characteristically very different, neither weaker nor stronger, and neither tried to be like the other. Most of all, I think Magaecian folklore portrayed women as the most spiritual and wise, deeply connected to nature and surprisingly courageous as Magae's protectors and guardians. Some say women were the heart of Mother Earth.

Myerscough taught magusic and magupe, which I also loved. It was a lesson to throw off all inhibitions and just sing, play or dance with a free spirit. Orford was annoyingly an exceptional dancer and quite brilliant on the fiddle too. I couldn't help but feel deep down that anyone capable of making an instrument sing in the way that he did, couldn't be all bad...but...we still had a vehement dislike of one another. We tried to get Mitchell to teach us silent spells but he always found a convenient excuse not to, so we got Letty to teach us as she seemed to get the hang of it from observing Mitchell and Myerscough, who were regularly in silent spell action. It took a bit of practice, but it meant that we could talk in lessons without being heard, so long as none of the teachers spotted us signing.

With the end of term drawing near, the cabin was looking very festive, donning shiny tinsel, gold and silver everywhere, and huge boughs of evergreens curled around doors and windows. A tall, fragrant pine tree stood proudly outside the cabin, an age-old resident of the land. It had been carefully decorated with fairy lights which were truly magical when night fell. A large placard hung over the cabin porch reading, MERRY GIFTMAS! It was a term Magaecians used often. It embraced all religions and races and implied that one should always cherish a time in the year for the gift of life and the chance to bring peace and goodwill to all men, no matter one's beliefs.

We set off early to spend the day exploring here for the last time before packing up to return to Quinton House where we'd get our final rainbow colours. We'd then continue on to the old Tribourne Hotel where our parents would be waiting to take us home for the Giftmas holidays. I'd never felt so connected as I had become to this place…an intense feeling of belonging, a freedom perhaps. In just a few months I'd recognised a new energy growing inside of me and I didn't want to let it go. I didn't want to lose the glorious melodies of birdsong or the friendly chatter of wildlife around me. I couldn't lose the smell of the earth as I drank her elixir of life from the brook across the way. It wasn't just me; I'm sure my friends sensed their own inner change too. Myerscough said we were *rewilding*, something all Dwellers should consider.

Each teacher, in their own way, taught us the value and power of words or spells. I got through loads of books here from the cabin library…mostly at night when my friends were sleeping as I still had a problem owning up to being a geeky book lover. I missed Mum and was excited to be seeing her again but I knew for sure I'd really miss it here and would need to return…like visiting, I imagine, your grandparents or any much-loved family member if you were lucky enough to have family.

"It's getting late, younglings," announced Myerscough. "We need to get back as we have a little end-of-term surprise waiting for you at the cabin."

"Let's have a race," suggested Mr Ademola. "We'll take the west route…Mrs Hayhurst can take the route that follows the brook and Mr Myerscough can take the old disused footpath."

"Good idea," replied Myerscough, shaking hands with the other teachers.

I was relieved that we wouldn't be returning through the Dweller fields of target-practice. We said our goodbyes to the wildlife, and thanked Magae for sharing her natural magic and beauty. It had started to snow, laying down a thin, white blanket as we set off behind Myerscough. Thomas walked in front with Kessie who was wearing a rose-tinted, pig-fitted fleece that made her look like a walking candyfloss. Thomas and Kessie had developed a special kinship like soulmates. Orford, of course, took every available moment to mock him, but Thomas didn't mind. I think he knew deep down that Orford was quite jealous of the affection he shared with his non-human friend. I must admit I was quite envious too as it reminded me of how much I'd been missing Lionel.

The walk took ages, each of my toes losing sensation until numbness meant that I couldn't feel the position of my feet against the ground. As I hadn't bothered to wear my woolly hat, the bitter wind painfully pierced my ears. "How much longer, sir?" I asked, puffing my words into little frozen clouds.

"Not long now," he snapped.

He was lying. It took another forty-five minutes. My lips had lost all feeling so that I was unable to articulate any words clearly enough to make any sense. I therefore decided not to complain but to keep quiet until the cabin eventually came into sight.

"What are they doing here?" growled Myerscough as we approached.

A group of menacing-looking men stood solid in front of the old oak door, their arms folded across their chests like a human barricade. They were dressed in dark coats like FBI agents or foreign super spies. I thought I recognised one of them from my first day at the Tribourne Hotel in Huckabee's office. It was Gibson Hastings, I was sure of it. Myerscough looked troubled at their presence. Kemp's face had become whiter than the falling snow.

"Hello, Ricky," said a large man, possibly even bigger than Myerscough. His hair was dark, as were his chiselled-out features. The man beside him, wearing a black beanie, was short and stocky with a wonky nose, which didn't look like it really belonged to his face.

"Ricky?" whispered Thomas. "That's rich. We could be Ricky and Sticky!" he sniggered.

"Preston," returned Myerscough, noticeably refraining from shaking the man's outstretched hand.

"Long time no see. How's the old shoulder?"

Myerscough growled under his breath. "What are you doing here? This is an E.S.S. You've no right to bring these men anywhere near us."

"We've come for Mr Pinkerton."

I looked across to Nyle. If his eyes had opened any wider, they might well have fallen out of their sockets. I moved over to him and grabbed his hand.

"Don't let them take me, Ellery…please…don't let them take me."

"You know the rules, Preston," said Myerscough. "These younglings are protected under the M.U.S.I.C."

"Yes…they were…until the agreement was broken, of course," he replied, forcing a newspaper into Myerscough's hand.

"I know nothing about this," said Myerscough, reading the headlines then tossing the paper to the ground behind him.

"Remove the boy," demanded Preston Hayes to his men.

"Wait!" yelled Myerscough, standing in front of us, his arms spread wide to shield us. "You need six men to remove a thirteen-year-old boy?"

Letty and I pushed Nyle behind us in the hope he wouldn't be seen. But it was no use. Six men descended on our unarmed teacher, making sure to hit him straight in his injured shoulder. They barged their way through us and grabbed Nyle, slapping Letty's hand loose. I closed my eyes and tightened my grip, which took every ounce of my strength, clenching both hands around Nyle's arm. They pulled the terrified boy, who was kicking and screaming as I, now joined by Thomas and Kemp, held fast to keep our grip firmly attached to Nyle. Delia ran towards us but slipped and fell, one of the men pushing her away roughly. Another man slapped Thomas hard, sending him backwards onto the snowy ground with a slippery thump. Kemp and

I held on relentless, Kemp's eyes tightly squeezed awaiting his blow...which came forcefully. The wonky-nosed man grabbed Nyle's arm then kicked me hard in the stomach, effortlessly releasing Nyle from my grip. My friend's distress was excruciating to watch. A tsunami of anger crashed through my innards as Nash's men dragged Nyle away.

"No! Leave him!" I screamed, clenching both fists by my side. One man instantly released his grip to cover his ears in pain, blood dripping through his fingers. I turned my attention to the other men who grabbed at their throats, unable to breathe, falling to their knees for mercy.

"Ellery!"

Myerscough startled me from my trance-like state to see the pain I'd inflicted on Nash's men. I was so confused. They deserved it, didn't they? And yet I felt unnerving remorse.

"Move!" roared Myerscough, grabbing Nyle by the arm and pushing him into us. "Into the cabin...all of you. I'll deal with this," he said, glaring at me in disappointment.

A whole term spent controlling my temper and redirecting it. Hour upon tedious hour of meditation, shapeshifting into my totem, namaste poses, and it had all gone out the window with the first encounter of trouble. I was no better than Nash and could see no way of changing that. As we walked slowly into the warm cabin lobby, the other two groups had caught up with us. Alarmed at the men's presence, Ademola and Hayhurst ordered their youngling groups inside to join us while the staff had a discussion outside. I watched Myerscough through the open door, rubbing his wounded shoulder as he retold the shocking events of Nyle's failed abduction. Although Nash's men had taken off without Nyle, they'd taken instead the knowledge that I was an ebonoid. It wouldn't be long before those six menaces would be returning for me and without using my negativity against them, I'd be heading straight for Nash, who would surely kill me, no questions asked.

Delia picked up the newspaper that Preston Hayes had thrown at Myerscough. She shared the headlines with us.

"Are you strong enough to implement the Burgess Manifesto after your Christmas dinner?" she began, before tearing off her gloves with her teeth. She placed one in each coat pocket, left then right. She cleared her throat and continued reading aloud.

"If humans are to survive, we need to reduce greenhouse gas emissions, and that means cutting right back on meat. Ignorance is no longer an excuse, people. It's time to stop sweeping those meat bones under your carpet and do something about it. Livestock—"

"I'm not listening to this," said Orford. "It's boring."

"It might seem boring to you, but Dwellers need to know this stuff," said Kemp, marching up and down on the spot, obviously still feeling cold.

"Basically," continued Delia, "it says here that we're losing all of our land by keeping so many cattle and that it's going to affect everything else in our ecosystem if we don't cut down on the amount of meat that we eat." She paused for a moment, then seemed to read it to herself.

"So people should just become vegetarians," said Thomas.

"I don't think it's as easy as that," I added. "I mean, people in poorer countries would suffer. Can I have a look, Delia?" I said, stretching out my hand for the newspaper. I knew the Burgess Manifesto already, but I wanted to see what the journalists were saying. Letty peered over my shoulder as I read the Manifesto's seven key points, then she read out the journalist's comments:

"...Animal welfare would improve as meat is produced not as a daily requirement but more as a treat.

Meat has always been of cultural importance – like turkey for Christmas, so this is not a removal but simply a reduction...although, let's face it, less is more! Let's be really radical, shall we? How about we create a more compassionate race as our New Year's resolution. Let's show more respect for our animal friends!

The upside is that less meat would mean better health; less disease and of course, less strain on our health service..."

As Orford stifled a yawn, Letty and I looked at each other. What the newspaper was saying was true, of course. I peered through the door again to see if the teachers had finished their discussion. They were still chatting. Myerscough was delving into his rucksack for something. He pulled out a large, brown envelope, the Burgess Manifesto envelope, and then everything that followed seemed to play out in slow motion. He opened the envelope and removed...the *Tribourne Monthly* magazine, then dropped his arms by his side with clenched fists. As he strode towards the cabin door, I knew I was in big, big trouble and started hyperventilating. Before I'd even put my shaking hands together in namaste, Myerscough had grabbed my arm and yanked me from the lobby, frogmarching me outside into the biting wind, well away from my friends to probably kill me...maybe not physically but definitely with an acerbic reprimanding spell.

"What's this?" he roared so violently I thought he might eat me.

"It's the *Tribourne Monthly*?" I squealed.

"I know it's the bloody *Tribourne Monthly*. Where's the Manifesto?"

I couldn't answer, so paralysed by fear I thought I might vomit.

He grabbed both my arms and lifted me off the ground so that our eye level was equal. "What have you done with it, Ellery?"

"I'm sorry," I cried. "I posted it through my next-door neighbour's door, the Kings, and then replaced it with the magazine on their doormat outside. They're politicians... they work in Westminster. I thought..." I was hyperventilating in terror. "I thought..."

"That's the one thing you didn't do, Ellery," said Myerscough, putting me down on terra firma. He looked so disappointed with my reply as he closed his eyes and pinched the bridge of his nose. He shook his large head in despair. "Have you any idea what you've done? Any idea how much danger you and all Magaecian children now face? You were all protected by the Magaecian Union, untouchable by Nash so long as the Manifesto remained unpublished. Now that you've broken that agreement all hell will break loose."

I wiped my painful tears, which had all but frozen to my cheeks. I drew in an icy breath for courage. "Why should it be only Magaecian children who are protected? All children have the right to protection, sir. Whatever Nash has been trying to achieve for all these years as head of the Magaecian Circle hasn't worked. Climate change affects everyone – that means Dwellers as well as Magaecians. I honestly can't see what I've done wrong here. I thought I was doing the right thing."

"You didn't think – you never do!" he shouted. "When are you going to learn to listen to your teachers, Ellery? This is not as simple as black and white. It's much more complicated than that," he hissed like a snake.

"Hendrick?" called Mitchell with a calming voice as he approached us. He paused as if thinking carefully before choosing the appropriate words to prevent Myerscough from thumping me one. "Sometimes children can see a much clearer picture than their seniors because to them, things are either right or wrong. There are no filters in between. To Ellery, the choice was a simple one. We can try to implement the Burgess Manifesto and have our lives endangered by Nash, or we can continue the way we are and have our species endangered by Magae." He raised his eyebrows in question, then nodded at me.

"Yes. I'd rather go for the first idea, or at least die trying," I said, my fists by my sides as I stood up as straight as I could. "We're all going to die with the second idea…and you know it, sir. Nyle said I have less to lose than most…but he's wrong. I have more to lose and that's why I'm more determined to go for it. If we don't go for it soon…it'll be too late. So if not now, then when? And if not me, then who, sir?"

Myerscough stood silent, his mouth ajar. I wasn't sure if he was going to hit me, shout at me or even swallow me whole. But he did nothing. Instead he glared at me then slowly closed his mouth and nodded. "I was wrong about you. You're not like your father at all. You're just like your uncle...a courageous bloody nightmare."

I took that as a compliment. If I were like my uncle, that must make me totally Hawk.

Myerscough sighed in resignation. "I knew you'd be trouble. If you don't get yourself killed, you'll get the rest of us killed."

Mitchell smiled, patted Myerscough on the back, then headed off to the cabin.

"Ellery, if you keep using that ebo force negatively, there will come a time...sooner than you imagine, when you'll stop feeling remorse at your actions and...you'll not be disturbed by the pain you cause. You will become worse than Nash himself...and there will be no return for you."

"Yes, sir."

"Next time anger strikes you, try imagining it like a negative ball within the pit of your stomach where the top side, facing upwards towards your face, is negative and the bottom side, facing your feet, is positive. Hold it tightly within you and physically turn it upside down so that the positive is on top. I've been told that this can actually be quite painful, but this pain means that you're holding onto your force and are in control of it so that you can change its use from negative to positive. The difficulty lies not in performing this task but in remembering to do it. Do you see?"

"Yes, sir. I think so."

"It's imperative that you never forget this, Ellery...and hopefully, given time, this should become second nature to you."

"Yes, sir."

"Now get going. It's the festive season, isn't it?"

I could hear magusic coming from the dining area. It was the folk music of the land, fun, light and rhythmic. The smell of mulled wine and oranges filled the air as I entered the dining room. The tables had been pushed to the outer walls, covered with festive food. Mince pies, gold-sprinkled chocolate brownies, pink and blue aquafaba meringues, festive donk, veg-filled puff pastries, nut loaves, brightly coloured curries – a feast to top all feasts. It was awesome and if you could be drunk on the atmosphere, then I was completely intoxicated. A collection of teachers played Magaecian folk instruments. Mr Ademola tapped a folk drum; Myerscough had joined them on the fiddle; Hayhurst on the banjo; Chef MacBrennan on the Irish flute; and her husband, Rory, on his uillean pipes. Nyle played his ukulele and Averil Harrington was on her concertina joined by Paige Livingstone on the tambourine. I danced merrily around the room with the remaining younglings and teachers. Thomas had a very natural rhythm on the floor, surprisingly at home in this new element. Letty, on the other hand, was so tall and gangly that her dancing was quite uncoordinated and she kept banging into people. Myerscough put down his violin and bounced to the centre of the floor, linking arms with dancing students, swinging them round. He linked my arm and danced with me, my legs off the ground as I held tightly to his muscular arm with both hands.

Thoughts of Nash catching up to murder me couldn't have been further from my mind as Myerscough passed a sensation of safety right through me. It suddenly dawned on me how lonely Nash must be…feared, not loved. Myerscough was right. This solitary vulnerability might provide the only route to his downfall. Myerscough let me down to link with other staff and students as we took it in turns to join arms with one another.

I caught a glimpse of Orford linking arms with Imogen and had an insane idea. I danced up to them, linked with Imogen, then with Orford. He immediately retracted, stopping dead in his dancing tracks at my gesture. I should have been angry and responded with a sassy spell or two but instead I yelled, "Dance off!" The music stopped and the staff looked bemused. Orford, knowing full well what a tremendous dancer he was and what a dreadful one I was, appeared bewildered at my request…but he nodded.

"You're on, Brown."

As the staff played a fast magusical gigue, Orford launched into a dance with the agility and poise of a gazelle, finishing with an impressive flying twist. He handed the floor over to me, confident of my failure to impress. I began with a fast step which resembled a sloth on caffeine. I started to laugh as I danced, as did my audience. Mrs Hayhurst had tears running down her face and some of my friends were holding their sides, unable to contain their laughter as I walked like an Egyptian, followed by flapping my arms and moving my head forward and back to show off my chicken walk. I finished with a flying swoop, landing elephant-style in a heap. I suppose I was making it funnier and funnier on purpose but I couldn't help it. Even Orford began to laugh as I handed the limelight back to him. We continued through the song, Orford performing a spectacular solo of steps and jumps before returning the floor to me once more but I couldn't continue. I was laughing far too much. I knelt down in mock worship. He truly was a wonderful dancer. As the whole room applauded in raptures, Orford gave me his hand, which I grabbed, rising to his eye level. He looked at me sternly before his face softened into a cheeky grin and a nod. He released my hand and walked over to his friends by the food table. I turned towards Myerscough, whose face was lit up with the proudest smile confirming that what might have been my worst day here had turned out to be my best.

15

ORFORD'S SECRET

I t was far too cold to be leaving this early in the morning. We said our goodbyes to the staff that remained, the MacBrennans who'd given each pupil a miniature festive donk to take home for the Giftmas break and Dr Ramsay, who had considerately fashioned individual chocolates in the shape of each youngling's totem. Delia Wu's parents had come to the cabin to whisk her off early for a family wedding in Edinburgh so we said our goodbyes to her too. Myerscough counted heads as we got ready in warm coats and hats to set off on foot to the jeeps heading back to Quinton House. He approached me with a book in his hand.

"Put this in your rucksack. At least I'll know where you are," he said, handing back *The Ebonoid, Dark and Light* with an uncharacteristic wink.

"Yes, sir," I replied, doing as he asked.

It was a long trek to the jeeps but on such a crisp and beautiful morning there were no complaints. Mr Mitchell was accompanying Myerscough in our jeep, Hayhurst had the company of Mr Wilberforce, and Ademola drove with Mrs Ball. Unlike my original journey to get here, I was wide awake for the journey back, taking in the scenery, chatting and singing festive songs. Even the usually stern Myerscough whistled along to "Jingle Bells". He taught us a Magaecian song called "The Vegg-nog Noel", which had at least twenty verses. As he and Mitchell competed over who could sing the loudest, they filled the car with positive energy, their deep voices bellowing out in bass baritone unison mixed with laughter when one or the other forgot the next verse.

The familiar sight of Hampstead Station came into view far quicker than I'd anticipated, which brought a giddy buzz to my insides at the prospect of being back home. The mood, however, suddenly changed as we approached the back gates of Quinton House, where there was a small courtyard for parking cars. Mitchell and Myerscough had become unnervingly silent. The two jeeps ahead of us were directed by a couple of men in smart coats to stop and park.

"Damn it!" cursed Myerscough under his breath.

I had no idea what had made him so agitated. Perhaps he was angry at having to wait outside the gates for his allotted parking spot. Patience was never his thing. I sat back in my seat thinking about what I'd do first when I got back to Tribourne. My thoughts halted abruptly on noticing Myerscough sending a silent spell to Mitchell. He spelled out *N, A, S, H…here*. I looked to my friends who saw it too, apart from Thomas, that is, who was still singing the chorus of "The Vegg-nog Noel". Letty nudged him into silence.

"What are we going to do?" I asked, unbuckling my seatbelt and moving forward to the two signing adults. "He's going to kill me."

"He's going to kill all of us," added Letty.

Mitchell looked surprised that we'd understood his silent spell but Myerscough seemed to have other, more worrying things on his mind. An official-looking black car, a BMW, I think, had come up behind us so we were wedged between the gates with nowhere to go but forward. Retreating was not going to be an option.

"Listen carefully, younglings. There's no time to repeat this," began Myerscough. "I'm going to pretend the car's not working…that it's conked out at the gate here so that I can block anyone coming in or out. Mr Mitchell can explain engine trouble out the front here to keep Nash's henchmen busy while I go round the back to…sort out the men in that car."

"Are you going to beat them up, sir?" asked Thomas.

"Mr Marks, Mr Myerscough will not be—" started Mitchell before being sharply interrupted.

"Yes, Thomas. I am."

"Cool!"

"Now when I say go…you whack the doors open to block the space even more and climb slowly out of the jeep. Mr Mitchell can say you're walking to the front of the building as we've blocked the way with our clapped-out vehicle."

We nodded nervously, knowing there was no time for questions.

"Head for the station down the hill. You'll be able to find it. Then go to Dave…you'll be safe there and it's only one or two stops from here. Disappear into the crowds. Don't draw attention to yourselves. Don't stop for anyone or anything or talk to anybody. Do I make myself clear?"

"Yes, sir," chanted my friends. I couldn't manage to get any words out.

"Do I make myself clear, Ellery?"

"But what about you?" I asked.

Myerscough smiled. "I appreciate your concern, Ellery, but he can't hurt me…I'm family."

"But—"

"No more time, Ellery."

"Here." Mitchell handed me his hag stone, the stone I had coveted at the beginning of term. The one I'd stopped myself from taking out of his desk. "It might protect you… from negative forces. You never know."

"I couldn't. I mean, it's yours. It found *you*."

"Well, it's found you now," growled Myerscough, snatching the stone impatiently. "Take the bloody stone. We haven't got time for this."

I nodded a *thank you* to Mitchell and put the stone in my pocket.

"Okay, boys and girls…here we go…" whispered Myerscough, followed by a huge intake of breath. He made the jeep bunny-hop to a standstill, then signalled for Mitchell to get out. "I'm going to the car behind. Go now."

We got out with our rucksacks and headed down the hill. I didn't turn to see if a punch-up had begun and neither did the others. We kept walking, silently and quickly with just one mission in mind – to get to Dave.

As the station came into sight, a surge of relief washed over me. We'd got over our first hurdle without being apprehended.

"We're being followed," whispered Kemp.

I turned my head back slightly to catch a glimpse.

"Don't look. He'll see you."

"It's not that wonky-nosed man, is it?" asked Letty. "He really frightens me."

"No," replied Kemp. "It's Nibley-Soames."

"Orford?" spluttered Nyle.

"Yes."

"That slimy, no-good rat," shouted Nyle, quickly shushed by Kemp. "He's going to grass on us and get us all killed."

I was so confused. I really thought I'd made a connection with Orford last night. I was furious but I wasn't about to let someone like him cause me to lose my composure, so I thought about the ball that Myerscough mentioned and captured my anger within my stomach before turning the ball upside down. A sudden blast of pain caused me to groan and double up as if I'd been winded.

"Ellery? What is it?" asked Nyle.

"It's nothing. I'm fine," I said, straightening up again.

"We'll have to lose him," said Kemp.

"We can't," I replied, raising my eyes in the direction of the station, which was almost in front of us. "We'll have to take him with us."

"Are you serious?" shrieked Nyle.

"Yes, I am. It's the only way. We'll hide inside the entrance. When he walks in looking for us, we'll jump him and interrogate him."

"Good idea," said Thomas, rubbing his hands together.

We walked into the station, then hid by the wall at the side of the ticket machine, waiting for Orford to appear. He came in, looking left and right before we pounced violently, pinning him to the wall, Thomas holding one arm and Kemp the other.

"About to rat us out, you stinking snitch?" screamed Nyle.

"No...no, it's not like that, I promise. I want to help you."

"Yeh...right," said Nyle sarcastically.

"Wait," I said, moving Nyle aside. "Why do you want help us, Orford?"

"Because...I've done something...something terrible."

"Have you killed someone?" asked Thomas, which caused us all to turn and look at our friend for asking such a dreadful question.

"I might as well have..." replied Orford, blinking his eyes tightly together to release a couple of tears.

"What have you done, Orford?" I asked, my stomach protesting at the uneasy sensation that I wouldn't like the reply he was about to give.

"Nash knows about the book...the one Myerscough used to find you."

"Right...better get rid of that, then," I said, looking back at Nyle before returning my gaze to Orford. "You're going to have to do better than that."

"I've been reporting to my dad once a week about school… about you being an ebo…about the book Myerscough gave to your mum."

I felt my jaw drop in horror. "Nash knows where my mum is?"

Orford nodded.

"Does Nash *have* my mum?"

He nodded again.

I covered my mouth and felt my warm tears drop over my cold fingers. "Has he…? Is my mum still…?"

"He hasn't killed your mum, Ellery, because…he won't kill her until he has you."

"I don't understand."

"He reckons the most painful torture for Nell would be to watch her child die an agonising death."

"Great."

"Mind you," said Letty, "while he hasn't got you, it means your mum's still alive, right?"

"Why the change of heart, Orford?" I asked in hope of a genuine answer.

"I dunno. It was after our Giftmas party last night, after that funny dancing. Hayhurst came up to me and said that Dwellers were actually no more than lost Magaecians."

"But Hayhurst hates Dwellers," I said curtly.

"No…her parents are Dwellers. She just thinks they're ignorant, that's all. Anyway, she said I should study my totem a bit more seriously and ask myself why it's a lizard."

"That seems obvious enough," said Nyle under his breath. "Cold-blooded reptile with shifty eyes."

I threw him a glare.

191

"A lizard can detach from its tail, which means I have the ability to let go of certain points of view. Things I've been taught, *forced* into believing all my life. Lectured time and again on all Dwellers being dangerous, wicked and harmful, rather than reaching my own conclusions. I think the lizard's my totem because it wants me to awaken my senses and break from my past. Maybe I should follow my own instinct…and not my parents'. I'm not going to be responsible for anyone's death…I'm not," he shouted. "Please…let me help you, Ellery."

"So how can you help us?" demanded Nyle, unconvinced.

"Give me the book and I'll take it as far as I can in the opposite direction. It might give you a little extra time before Nash catches up with you. He will catch up with you though, you know that, don't you?"

"Nash will catch up with you too, Orford…if you do this. He might well kill you when he finds out what you've done. You're the son of two members of the Magaecian Circle."

"I know…but it doesn't matter. Besides…I'm a lizard. I can regenerate."

"Only your tail," I replied as I took out the book and handed it to Orford.

"How can we trust him?" asked Nyle.

"That's easy," I replied with a smile. "You're going with him."

"I'm what? No way."

"He's your cousin. You can catch up on lost family time." I unhooked my elephant earrings from my freezing ears and passed one to Nyle and the other to Orford. "Here. The elephant totem will protect you. It's never let me down." I cuddled Nyle, wondering whether it might be the last time I'd see him if Nash caught up with me. Orford awkwardly held out his hand for a handshake, which I ignored, going straight in for a hug instead, which he returned.

"Thank you...both of you. I'll never forget this."

16

CLASH OF THE TOTEMS

We arrived at a very different-looking Beaulieu Gardens as living rooms were lit up with Christmas trees and Dave's door was strewn with holly. We rang frantically on Dave's doorbell but there was no reply. We kept ringing and knocking but there was no answer.

"She's not in," puffed Thomas, peering through her letterbox.

"Yes, I am," replied Dave back through the letterbox, laughing. She opened the door. "It takes a while for old people to get down the stairs, you know. Merry Giftmas, children."

"Dave!" I ran into her arms and sobbed. "He's got my mum. What are we going to do? I'm not going to be able to take on a power like that. I can't beat him."

"Hush now. Of course you can't take him on...not alone." She smiled, looking at my three friends.

"He's not going to kill Ellery's mum until she watches Ellery die an agonisingly slow and torturous death," said Thomas, prompting Letty to nudge him hard in the ribs.

"Let's figure this out with a hot chocolate," said Dave, calmly walking us into her kitchen, which smelled of cinnamon. "I can teach you how to unite your totems. Nash fights alone. He might have enormous power in his snake totem but his lack of allies is his greatest weakness. You must work together. This will give you strength."

We followed the old lady into the warmth of her living room and sat by the curling flames of the flickering fire, comforted by its gentle heat.

"You know how to call upon your totems," she said. "Place your totem stones in your hands, then once you're together, sharing your totem's energy as one, you can use your animal senses and instincts to receive and unite with the other totem animals around you. You'll sense their presence even if you are unable to see them."

We began our meditative journey to unite with our totems. We'd done it so many times now back at the cabin, always carrying our totem stones, which we'd made with Mitchell and Mrs Ball, in our pockets like part of our Quinton School uniform. I exited my cave onto a grassy field where the honey badger was waiting for me. I felt it share its power as I screamed out the gruff *raa-raa-raa* sound that they make. I became immediately unafraid as a I linked with a species with not many natural predators. My skin was thick and I could defend ferociously. I felt my short but sturdy legs and extremely tough claws, so long on my front limbs. As I tried movement with my short tail, I steadied myself with my heavily padded soles. I looked around for the elephant, which was always with me…but it was absent, nowhere to be seen. My stomach tightened. The elephant was my guardian and yet it was gone when I needed it most. I inhaled to clear my head, replacing my panic with reassurance, concluding that it must have followed Nyle and Orford. As I continued my meditation a large pig stood beyond me, sturdy and strong and a heron flew down to land on the pig's back for a moment before flying off again. I couldn't see Kemp's mouse but I could definitely sense its presence as I heard Dave's faint voice in the distance.

"Children, come back. There's trouble. You need to get yourselves out of here."

We came back out of our meditation and into Dave's living room with a bit of a start as she busily collected up our hot chocolate mugs.

"They're coming," she said, raising her eyes to the street outside her living room window.

A black electric BMW was pulling up outside Dave's house. How she'd managed to notice its silent arrival was baffling. She removed a totem stone from within her sari. Embossed with a black raven, she held it tightly in her hand.

"Go through the kitchen into the back garden, then get yourselves over the fence and into the adjoining garden behind. They have a large garden gate that exits to the road. Hurry now."

As we sped off through the kitchen door, Dave's doorbell rang, accompanied by violent fists banging on her street door. Dave was deliberately taking ages to answer, giving us just enough time to disappear out of view. We climbed over her garden fence, none more nimbly than Thomas, who had become quite fit over the last few months. My stomach lurched with an overwhelming nausea, possibly from over-indulging on hot chocolate, but more likely from the anguished thoughts entering my head over Dave's safety once Nash's men found out that we'd been there…and that she'd helped us.

We headed once more for Wembley Station.

"What now?" asked Letty, as if I'd have some ingeniously concocted idea.

"I'm going to have to go back to Quinton House."

"Are you mad?" cried Kemp.

"Nash has my mum. I've got to help her, Kemp. I reckon if Nash is in Hampstead, chances are my mum is too."

"You can't challenge him alone, Ellery. You heard Dave," started Thomas. "You need us…we're coming with you…right?" he asked, turning to the other two.

"Right," they replied.

***

We sat on the tube to Hampstead Station in nervous silence. Trying to be as inconspicuous as possible, we walked up the hill until turning into the road where Quinton House was in view in all its imposing architectural glory.

"We're never going to get in there unseen," said Kemp. "Look at the size of that bloke guarding the door. He's bigger than Myerscough."

"Probably waiting for us," added Thomas. "Waiting to catch us and torture us."

"Come back here!" yelled a woman, taking the enormous man with her as he opened the gate, racing through it in hot pursuit of a ginger cat being chased by a dog.

"Lionel?" I uttered.

"Now's our chance," whispered Kemp.

"What about Lionel?" I said.

"He'll be fine," said Letty, doing her best to sound reassuring. "He's always fine. Besides…he's probably a lot safer out here than in there. Come on, it's our only chance."

We bolted through the open gate then crept through the back of the building to the library, which was empty and dark.

"Shhh…someone's coming," whispered Kemp.

We slid under Crawford's desk and held our breath.

"Move!" yelled a gruff voice from the corridor outside.

I peeked round the edge of the desk to see a young boy's legs walking past, followed by another boy who tripped over from a probable push from his captor. He looked my way and saw me. I gripped my mouth with both my hands to stop myself from crying out as I recognised Orford. He and Nyle obviously hadn't got very far with the book. Orford's face twitched nervously as he got to his feet promptly to avoid anyone looking our way.

Once they'd left, we crawled from the desk to see them disappear into the dining area. We looked about us for unwanted henchmen, then, satisfied the coast was clear, we sneaked out of the library and through the open dining hall door, keeping hidden behind the stacks of chairs at the back of the room. At the front of the large dining hall was Nash. I'd never met him but I knew it instantly to be him. He was tall and broad with a sculptured face of such striking beauty, it took my breath away. His face was the one in the ebonoid book…and there was no doubt that it also belonged to the boy in Myerscough's photo. They must've grown up together.

Nyle and Orford were practically flung at his feet, which averted my eyes to a stout woman's body lying motionless to the side of him. Mrs Huckabee? She barely stirred, moving spasmodically. A dishevelled Mitchell was shielding the Year 8s together with Ademola and Hayhurst, whose normally short, tidy-styled hair was all over the place, resembling a poorly built bird's nest, frizzing out in all directions. My heart dropped, catching sight of Myerscough, one eye almost closed, swollen and bruised and one shoulder hanging loosely by his side, more than likely dislocated again. Four muscly men stood over him, ready to restrain him should he want to make a move.

"Not one but *two* children of Magaecian Circle members have dared to conspire against our people," roared Nash. His voice was deep, almost melodic in a macabre sort of way. *"You!"* he shrieked at Orford, forcing him to his feet. "Where is the girl?"

"I don't know, sir." Poor Orford trembled before being dealt a large dose of negative ebonoid anger. Orford screamed out in pain, falling distressed to his knees. I clenched my fists to try my level best to hold the negative energy brewing within me. I pictured the ball and slowly turned it upside down, making me groan in pain.

"It looks like your friend will have to divulge then, or you'll feel my impatient rage once more. Where is the girl, Pinkerton?"

Nyle stood up, his whole body twitching and trembling. "I-I don't know either, sir." Nyle shut his eyes tightly, no doubt waiting for Nash to deliver a blast of great pain, but a bloodcurdling scream emanated from Orford, now gasping for breath as Nash punished him instead.

Nyle stood rigid in terror.

"Hold it, Ellery," whispered Kemp. "You must hold it in."

I held my negative feelings with clenched fists, forcing myself to physically invert the negative ball in my stomach. The pain was so intense I was struggling to breathe. The after effect, however, was one of strength...great positive strength.

Nash signalled something to a man who went off, returning promptly with a woman, bedraggled and hardly capable of walking without aid. Her loose, lank hair was stuck to her face, which she tried to remove in slow, strained strokes. As her features became visible, my heart squeezed hard within my chest. The blood stopped circulating round my body as it swallowed up fragments of my shredded vital organ at the sight of my poor, broken mother. She was hardly recognisable. I took my anguish and held it more and more tightly, turning that ball within me. It was almost impossible to keep my pain quiet, it hurt so very much.

"I'll ask again, Mr Pinkerton. Where is the girl?"

Orford shook his head at Nyle.

"I don't know, sir."

He hit Orford again. His agonising cry was excruciating to my ears. This cruel man then turned on Nyle, who jolted his head back in painful distress. I couldn't bear to watch. I repeated my exercise, unable to hold back my tears, drawing on every ounce of strength within me to hold the anger and channel it away from negativity. The pain was so intense, I fell to my knees and shut my eyes tightly, blinking large salty droplets onto the floor. If it got any worse I'd be unable to cope. As the pain passed it left me with a strange positive strength, but this wasn't going to be enough to save my mum or my friends. There were no more options for me. I was going to die whatever I did so I reckoned I might as well die trying to do the right thing...face Nash while I was still capable of standing upright.

I reached for my totem stone in my pocket and felt the hag stone too. I took the deepest breath, holding it for almost a minute, before letting it out. I clenched both stones and nodded...I was going.

"No!" whispered Letty, trying to grab me.

"There's no other way, Letty. I have to do this. I have to." Rising unsteadily to my feet and moving away from the stack of chairs, I let out a blusterous roar.

"Stop!" Placing my hands together around my stones in namaste to remain in control but unthreatening, I headed to the front of the room. "I'm here now, you bully. You can stop."

"No, Ellery," croaked Mum, who was hit by another of Nash's forceful blasts as a result of her outburst.

Thomas ran up behind me, shouting, "Wait! You can't hurt her. She's your daughter. She's family...and you can't hurt family. It's an unsaid rule."

An audible gasp filled the air but Nash just let out an evil laugh of satisfaction. On the plus side, while he was laughing, he wasn't blasting anyone with pain.

"This is just too delicious," he said, smiling smugly. "I'm not your father. Is that what you think...because you're an ebonoid?"

"Because my mother was your girlfriend."

"Oh dear, Ellery. It *is* Ellery, isn't it?"

I didn't acknowledge his question, tightening my hands together.

Namaste won't help you here, my dear ebo. You won't be able to control yourself when you find out the truth...who your father really is."

I stood in silence, completely baffled as to where he was going with this.

"Your mother was my girlfriend...oh yes, because I needed her to be. Needed her to reveal what was in her brother's bloody Manifesto to me. It was my mission to avoid that Manifesto's presentation to the Magaecian Circle. It wasn't worthy of a Magaecian audience, particularly as the author was not even Magaecian – only too apparent in the content of his Manifesto, which defies all Magaecian beliefs. I'd never have *relations* with his sister, a repulsive, repugnant Dweller. Besides, her infatuation with me was merely temporary as she was clearly in love with another. I was a fool. I underestimated her intelligence as she double-crossed me, using me as I had used her, uncovering my plans to topple her brother from his position as head of the Magaecian Circle. Nell should've gone up in flames with the rest of her family. I should've known that Darwin would compose a plan to separate himself from the document to assure its safety. I should have killed her when I had the chance...but she disappeared. I had no idea she was pregnant or that she would hide with her child, conveniently safe for thirteen years. It looks like those years have finally caught up with you, Nell," he bellowed, throwing another negative blow her way. Her screams tore right through me as if he'd dealt the pain straight to me. I grasped my distress and held it, turning it upside down before crying out.

"Well done. That's very good, Ellery," said Nash sarcastically. "I wonder who taught you that," he continued, looking over at Myerscough. "It's all to do with genetics, you see. The ebonoid gene runs in the Nash line. The Nash family all carry the gene but few will have the actual ebonoid trait. An ebonoid parent would never be able to produce an ebonoid child as there's a possibility they might kill each other. No…it misses many generations before the trait resurfaces. You see, my father, Wyndham Nash and his sister, Florence, were both carriers. Aunt Florence married the handsome Dwennon – Dwennon Myerscough – and produced a lovely bouncing bundle of joy called Hendrick…a carrier of the ebonoid gene, a gene that's actually immune to the pain that's induced by my physical ebonoid negativity."

I stood motionless, my mouth ajar as I tried to process this staggering information.

"Have you never wondered why your temper has no effect on Mr Myerscough? Why he's never nervous around you? Ever wondered why I can't punish him in the same ebonoid way I punish deserving others?" He narrowed his eyes at me, awaiting my reply, which was not forthcoming as I stared back, still stunned, in silence. He produced a disturbing smile, filling me with a paralysing terror. "It seems I can destroy him now though, and his Dweller partner, by killing the one person they hold most dear. I'm afraid it needs to be as slow and as painful as possible, of course…for me to get maximum satisfaction, you understand? No hard feelings, I hope?"

"You can do what you like. You've still lost, Simeon."

"What did you call me?" snapped Nash, sending a foreboding vibration around the room. A couple of Year 8s fainted.

"I looked up your name…your *real* name. Simeon means *he who listens*. Perhaps that's why your parents chose it. Maybe they hoped that one day their son might become head of the Magaecian Circle, and as a good and worthy leader he'd listen to the needs of his people. I'm guessing you lost that ability the moment you lost your name. You've been head of the Circle for thirteen years and yet you haven't achieved anything. Magae couldn't be any worse off. Climate change, global warming, greenhouse gas emissions through the roof. If you were going to have a positive effect on your people, you'd have done it by now. But you can't, can you? You don't know how to be positive. A friend told me…a good friend, it turns out… that Dwellers are simply lost Magaecians. Well…the only lost Magaecian I can see…is *you*. So very lost, so very far from the true essence of respecting our fellow man, hearing, not dictating in our attempt to heal Magae and remain on her planet. So if you want to destroy my mother and my…father," I said, looking across to Myerscough with a smile, "then give it your best shot. The Manifesto is out, no longer concealed and you can't do anything about that. Dwellers will begin to follow it, slowly but surely. I guess that makes it win-win for me no matter what you do and…lose-lose for you, cousin."

Nash's beautiful face contorted in rage. "Enough! How dare you."

I looked up at his crimson complexion and kept my hands together. "I'm not frightened of you."

"You should be. I'm going to hurt you with more pain than you ever thought humanly possible. And then...when you beg for me to stop and kill you...I'm going to hurt you some more."

"Oh yeah? Then what are you waiting for? Bring it on, cuz!"

"Your totem, Ellery!" cried out Myerscough.

I plunged my bottom to the floor, my hands still together in front of me, then closed off the noise to meditate super fast. I darted through my cave and into the open field where my honey badger stood waiting to share its spirit and its power. A trusty dog stood by me. I think it was Nyle's totem, brave and consistent, protective and devoted to his family and friends. Nash's snake, so dark and hideous like an evil column covered in onyx scales of armour, descended upon me with a venomous attack. Its jaws opened wide to penetrate my flesh with its long pointy fangs, two thin needles full of poison. Its head held back for a moment, hissing loudly before it lunged at me full force...then again, but its attempts were thwarted by my loose skin. Nash wasn't going to surrender that easily and as he repeatedly struck me, over and over, I was all too aware that he'd probably pierce my skin eventually and inject me with a lethal dose to finish me off slowly and painfully as the venom took hold. As I tried my best to battle with this oversized serpent, a large, wild pig moved in front of my body to take full punishment.

Pig skin is fortuitously tough to bite through so I was pretty confident that it would be okay for a little while at least, until Nash's tail coiled around the pig, squeezed, then threw him a serious distance to land, injured, against a tree. The time to plan my next move was a luxury I didn't have. I racked my brain to remember my teachings but it was as if someone had pressed delete and wiped everything clean. It was too late as black coils encased me, squeezing the life out of me. As I exhaled, the coils tightened more and more, stopping me from breathing in. But Nash's totem was supposed to be a venomous snake, not a constrictor. The DNA of honey badgers meant that I was immune to most snake venom. I'd researched it. I'd done my homework for Mitchell, so why was this happening? Was I about to be squished to death? Death by squishing…was that even a thing?

I couldn't breathe and could feel my life slipping away as my surroundings blurred. Out of the corner of my eye, I spotted a small indistinct shape scuttle in front of the snake. It was a little mouse. The snake was unable to ignore its instinctive nature to eat and digest the mouse, which would take a lot less time and effort than a honey badger. It released its grip, just enough for me to breathe in. As it dislocated its massive jaws it pounced on the mouse to gulp it down whole. My friend's rodent body bulged beneath the snake's scales but my broken skeleton was unable to stand as I still gasped for air. While mustering the little energy left in my body in another attempt to stand, an elephant swept past me and stamped hard with its foot on the snake. The mouse was instantly regurgitated out of the snake's muscular jaws and flew through the air, where it was caught by a passing heron to take it to safety. The snake, unable to move, spun round its head to stab the elephant sharply in the ankle with its fangs. The elephant let out a high-pitched shriek as it faltered, then fell stiffly with its whole body weight onto the snake, squashing it so hard that its eyes bulged out of its head, glassy and lifeless. As I took a closer look, a white orb of light released itself from the snake's open mouth. It hovered for a moment or two before heading straight for my chest, a bolt of lightning hitting me like a white-hot poker. The searing pain was so intense I couldn't bear it. I screamed out in such crippling torment. I wanted to die so that the pain would be over. A crushing darkness descended upon me as if someone had ripped out my eyes.

"Ellery! Ellery…"

I opened my eyes to see a blurry image of the Quinton House dining room and Myerscough limping fast towards me, the torn hem of his trousers caked in blood as he left a magenta trail behind him. I was disorientated, dizzy with pain as I attempted to get to my feet. As I swayed on my unstable legs, a second all-consuming strike hit my insides with such a force, I knew it wouldn't be long before I was spent.

"Don't let go, Ellery!" screamed Myerscough. "Finish what your uncle started. Do you hear me? You are so very much like him, Ellery. He never gave up…and neither will you."

*Just like my uncle…just like my uncle…*those words, those spells filled my whole being with such a positive vibration that I clung to it as tightly as I could…and then some. If Nash killed me now, at least I'd finally discovered who I was.

I was Ellery Burgess-Myerscough. ELLERY BURGESS-MYERSCOUGH. I was totally Hawk! My surroundings grew ever more chaotic as they blurred into a blanket of silent blackness...

17

FINDING THE LOST MAGAECIANS

"Ellery, my baby…open your eyes."

My eyelids didn't want to move, still in overdrive to protect my eyes from further horror.

"Ellery…"

The tenderness in the voice was familiar as my senses rebooted. The air held a warm odour of toast and jam with a touch of antiseptic thrown in. My eyelids gave a flutter as they rose up into a lazy squint.

"Are we all dead?"

Mum covered her mouth to hide her grin. "You're in hospital."

I rubbed my eyes to fully focus on the young, familiar faces surrounding my bed. Letty, Kemp, Nyle…and Orford.

"Where's Thomas?" I asked, concerned that my fattest friend had met with a terrible end.

"Don't fret," replied Myerscough, "Sticky's down in the fracture clinic. He broke his wrist."

"Why do you always call him that? He risked his life for me. He deserves a bit more respect...sir," I responded indignantly.

"Isn't it obvious, Ellery?"

I shook my head, which was a mistake as it felt as though a stampede of wild horses must have trampled all over it while I'd been unconscious.

"Because...he *sticks* to his friends."

I opened my mouth to come back with a sarcastic retort before realising that I didn't need to. He was right... he really did stick to his friends. I gazed at Myerscough's bruised and battered face, narrowing my eyes. "I think I might have been a bit delirious...but I imagined that Nash said that he wasn't my father...*you* were. Was I hallucinating?"

"Not a hallucination...a fact." He smiled broadly, reaching over to embrace me, which hurt like hell and yet comforted me in a strange sort of way.

"So your totem's the elephant, isn't it?" I asked.

He nodded.

"How come the venom didn't kill you?"

"It's genetic. The gene makes me immune."

"Right." I smiled. "What happened to Nash?"

Myerscough glanced anxiously across to Mum. "He's gone."

"Gone...dead...gone?" I asked. "Or gone...for now, gone?"

"I'm not going to lie to you, Ellery. The truth is, I don't

really know. That light that came from Nash…that burned into your chest…"

"I thought it was going to kill me."

"Hmmm, there was a moment I thought it was going to kill you too."

"Was that Nash's ebonoid force shifting through to join mine? I mean, will I now become…?"

"That was Nash's essence in a last-ditch attempt to remove your force to join with his own and defeat you."

"You mean…kill me?"

"Yes…I suppose so. It's what an ebonoid does…an ebonoid out of control, that is. But as I've told you on more than one occasion, a positive energy is much stronger than a negative one. It seems that, for whatever reason, he couldn't attach to your energy…so the answer to your question is… no, you haven't acquired any of his force and you should never become like him…so long as you stay in control."

"I don't understand," I replied. "I thought two ebonoid couldn't exist together. Only one can survive and in so doing, gain the other's power."

"Yes, that's right…but that only applies to a physical negative force. All people, Magaecians and Dwellers alike, have positive and negative energy within them but an ebonoid is able to produce his or her negative energy physically. It is this energy that a rival ebonoid will strive to obtain."

"But surely you'd want the negative energy to be removed…so it's a good thing, isn't it?"

"No, it's never a good thing because attached to your negative life force is your positive life force. It can't be separated no matter how big or small it might be. Removal of one is

211

removal of both. Removal of both is removal of life in any form. If he's able to latch onto the negative part of your life force, he will consume your very self so that you are no more. The fact that he failed means that you must've produced an incredibly positive energy there, Ellery. But I'm afraid his powers were exceptionally strong, so potent and intense that it's unlikely they've been completely dissolved. I'd like to think you defeated him but I suspect you just surprised him… shocked him, really. He wasn't prepared for you to react in the way that you did. He expected you to fight in the way that he does, using negative ebonoid power, which understandably from you, would have been only too feeble. A teenage girl would've been no match for the mighty Nash."

"But the snake was dead."

"Yes…the snake was dead but Nash will most likely find another totem if he eventually recovers."

"Do you think he'll come back to get me?"

"That depends on you, Ellery."

"On me?"

"Nash needs a negative energy to latch on to…so you mustn't give him that opportunity. You'll have to control your temper and channel it intelligently. Always find the source of your anger, then you will find your solution. See all sides to every argument. Open your eyes to how closely connected we all are. Find what unites us rather than what makes us different."

"I'm not sure I'll be able to do all that forever, sir."

"Ellery…if you've managed to live through the episode you just have…then I reckon it will be plain sailing from here on in, my girl."

It definitely wasn't going to be plain sailing from here on in…and he knew it…but perhaps the more positive you were, the more positive you'd be, if that made any sense?

"Besides," continued Myerscough, casting an affectionate glance at my friends, "one thing you have that Nash doesn't…is us…*all* of us. Love and kindness will always be stronger than violence and anger. I don't think Nash should be something you need worry about at this moment in time."

I gave a cynical nod, which I halted almost immediately as my head felt like an eggshell ready to crack at any moment. All I really wanted to do was sleep.

***

I was allowed home for Giftmas Day in Tribourne. Poor Orford had been disowned by his parents for opposing Nash so he was staying with his cousin, Nyle. It turns out that he was given a violet on his E.S.S. rainbow for outstanding bravery in the face of mortal danger. It must have taken a great deal of courage not only to stand up to Nash but to stand up to his parents like that. We'd all done pretty well with our rainbows, with most of Myerscough's tutor group highly commended for *exhibiting exceptional totem ingenuity*.

Mum and Myerscough – it was going to take a while before I felt comfortable calling him Dad – looked as though they'd been in a fight with a fire-breathing dragon…and lost. Myerscough wore his rugged cuts and bruises well and although Mum looked frail, her eyes were bright, like a flame had reignited in her soul. I was comforted by the happiness and hope she radiated. This was something I'd never seen before in my mum. Even her face seemed less creased, less worried, gentler somehow.

I was excited to experience my first Giftmas as a complete family unit. I still found Myerscough a little scary but he was a hundred times less scary than Nash whom I'd originally believed to be my father. Myerscough brought a goose for lunch – not to eat, but to run round the garden with Kessie and Lionel, who incidentally, was found sitting quietly on Hampstead Heath after his escape from Quinton House. Thomas and his mum joined us for lunch, which was a traditional festive Magaecian meal that Mum had found from Myerscough's book, *Mealish Made Simple*.

"Mr Myerscough, sir…"

Myerscough raised his eyebrows laughing.

"I mean, Dad, sir…I mean, just…Dad?"

"What is it, Ellery?"

"What's going to happen now…with Nash gone?"

"With any luck, the Burgess Manifesto will be implemented and slowly but surely, with a bit more luck, we might still have a chance of survival on Magae…so long as we have the right people on the Circle," he replied with a mouthful.

"Mr Myerscough?" asked Thomas. "Or perhaps I should call you…Ricky?"

"Or perhaps you shouldn't if you want to live until New Year," snapped Myerscough.

"Right."

"Spit it out then, boy," growled Myerscough.

"Are you going to ask Ellery's mum to marry you now?"

"Thomas!" shrieked his mother. "You can't ask people personal questions like that."

"It's okay, Prunella." Myerscough laughed. "The fact is…Ellery's mum and I are already married."

"What?" I jumped up from my seat but sat down again quickly when Myerscough fixed an unblinking gaze on me.

"You see…when Nell's family were killed, we fled. It seemed all too clear that our days were numbered. Nash was coming for us…we had the Manifesto, after all. We couldn't even stay for the funerals if we were to get out of the country…"

I looked across to my mum who was nodding in agreement while wiping tears from her cheeks.

"We flew to Sri Lanka, where Dave's nephew, Amesh, took us to an army barracks. From there we flew on a tiny aircraft to the south to stay with Amesh's wife's family who looked after us for a couple of months…probably the best months of my entire life. It was here that we married with a small ceremony laid on by the local villagers. It was idyllic, such a long way from all the troubles we'd left behind. During the ceremony, the strangest thing happened. An elephant walked across the sand in front of us."

"Your totem," dribbled Thomas with a mouthful of gravy.

"Yes, indeed. It was a sign…a sign of the long, hard journey ahead for me and the strength I would need from my totem to take care of my family. We didn't know how bad things had become back home. People were disappearing, hiding or *being removed*."

"You mean killed?" asked Thomas.

"Yes."

"Cool!"

Myerscough returned Thomas's inappropriate remark with an unrelenting scowl, which instantly silenced him.

"It wasn't long before word got out that Nell and I were in Sri Lanka. I don't know how Nash got wind of it but we both knew it would be certain death if he found us...and he *would* find us."

"So what did you do?" I asked.

"Your mum found out that she was pregnant so there was only one thing I could do..."

We all looked at him in silent anticipation, holding our breath.

"Let him catch me so that I could save my wife and unborn child. Poor Nell must've thought I'd done a terrible thing. I left her a note...I wouldn't have been able to say it convincingly to her face. It said that I'd made a terrible mistake and that I shouldn't have married her. It said... she shouldn't come looking for me...I didn't love her." Myerscough choked on his words, stroking his stubble when he was clearly catching his tears. "I told her to change her identity for her and the baby's safety. I hoped in my heart that if I did miraculously survive, I'd come back and find her...if she didn't hate me for what she thought I'd done."

"So why didn't you?" I asked. "Didn't you want to see what I looked like? You missed every birthday...every milestone..."

"Of course I wanted to know what my child looked like... to know what it felt like to hold you. Of course I yearned for my wife. She was the love of my life...but..." He took a large swig of red wine before continuing. "But it wasn't safe. Nash wanted possession of the Manifesto...which I'd secretly posted to Aldora Huckabee. When he and his men ambushed me at Gatwick Airport, I knew he wouldn't kill me until I either handed it over or made a deal with him."

"To leave all the children at the E.S.S. untouched under the M.U.S.I.C. in return for never opening the Burgess Manifesto…"

"Exactly. Very good, Ellery. This meant that whether I found you or not, I could at least keep you safe."

"But I don't understand. Why didn't you come back for us once you'd made the deal?"

"Because Nash wasn't satisfied with *just* the deal. He was obsessed to the point of insanity to find your mother, who had been one of the few people to ever successfully double-cross him. He wasn't going to rest until he'd got her and had his revenge, despite getting what he wanted…becoming head of the Magaecian Circle. This obsession was clouding his judgement and powering up his ebonoid negativity to a dangerously unhealthy level."

"So why did you return to the city where Nash might find us, Mum?"

"Because it was so obviously unsafe that I guessed he wouldn't suspect it. Your grandparents had a flat in the city that they bought many years ago before Darwin was born. They'd never used it themselves, always choosing to stay in a London hotel or with me or Darwin when they were away from Ireland. It was just an investment to rent out for extra cash. When Mum and Dad were killed, the flat automatically became mine. Nash knew nothing about it so I was safe… for a while anyway. I thought your dad was gone for good so I dedicated my life, 24/7 to my baby, keeping you safe for as long as I possibly could. Things in the city were changing and I knew it was time to move on. That's why we moved to Tribourne. I thought we'd be safer in a more rural area."

"If we didn't die of boredom first," I muttered under my breath. "So how did you know we'd moved here?" I asked, turning to Myerscough.

"I didn't. I got lucky. I searched endlessly, scouring the countryside for you and your mum but got nowhere. I'd almost given up when Nash began displaying an unhealthy interest in Tribourne. He kept sending Circle members up here so I suggested that Tribourne Village should be where Quinton E.S.S.'s autumn term should begin. The only school I found in the village was Saint Timothy's, so I researched the staff list to find the school librarian, Nuala Brown. Brown's a very common name, of course, but it was Nell's mother's maiden name. Nash wouldn't have known this but I did… and Nuala's an Irish name, probably the closest sounding name to Nell…also something only I might pick up on." He took Mum's hand in his and smiled lovingly at her, which put me off my lunch a bit. "When Saint Timothy's was burned down, it was clear that Nash was getting uncomfortably closer to finding Nell. I don't think he knew about you, which is why you were always going to be safer with me at school than with your mum."

I nodded. It was difficult to digest all of this new information. I was always so angry at my dad for not being around for me. I think perhaps I still was in a way. I felt cheated of all the years that I'd missed with a dad. It was irrational, I know, especially as Myerscough had let himself get caught, risking an almost certain death to save both me and Mum. I mean, the poor man was unspeakably tortured. He'd apparently not had a proper night's sleep in thirteen years because of it.

"Anyway," said Myerscough, glugging down the last drop of wine in his glass. "I can't give you back the birthdays I've missed, Ellery…but I can be here for the birthdays to come." He smiled, then got up from the table, retrieving his fiddle and also my flute…which wasn't technically a flute at all, but a fife. An old Myerscough family heirloom.

"Both mums can clap along while young Sticky here gives us a lively gigue."

I took a sip of vegg nog which slid down my throat with a creamy loveliness, then tuned up with Myerscough…I mean, my dad…and watched my fattest, stickiest friend dance round the kitchen, knocking over various ornaments with his wrist, which was wrapped in a bright green cast. Kessie danced a pig gigue and Lionel barked in rhythmic bursts as he tried to catch Kessie's curly tail.

As both mums got up to join in the dancing, the sensation of happiness running through my every vein was like a current of new life. I felt whole for the first time. I finally knew who my father was, not just a name or a face, but a personality in the flesh. There was no doubt this man was terrifying but he was also seriously and totally Hawk! I honestly hoped the world would change now that the Manifesto was out. It was possible….it really was. And even if Nash did return, no one should want to follow him because maybe, at least maybe by then, all those lost Magaecians…would be found. Okay…so that's a bit cheesy and a touch naive…but it was to be a new beginning, a second chance for Dwellers and Magaecians to show Magae that we really could respect her planet, that we really were worthy to remain.

And Nash? I suppose I'd have to face him again one day, wouldn't I?

18

DONK

MAGAECIAN DONK
(CHEF MACBRENNAN's FOOD SPELL)

Ingredients
- 2 cups Bran Flakes
- 1 cup raisins/sultanas
- 1/4 cup coconut sugar (or maple syrup)
- 2 cups plant milk (oat milk or almond milk work best but you can try others)
- 2 cups self-raising flour (wholewheat's healthier)

The spell
Put all of the ingredients EXCEPT FOR THE FLOUR into a bowl.
- Mix and leave for about an hour.
- Mix in the flour and pour the mixture into an

oiled loaf tin (add a little more milk if the mixture becomes too dry).

- Bake for about 45 minutes at 180°C (or until an inserted knife comes out clean).
- Leave to cool before turning upside down and cutting.
- Share with Magaecians and Dwellers!

ACKNOWLEDGEMENTS

'm not going to list all the many books I've read or the incredible people who have given me the knowledge that I needed to truly understand our planet's dilemma. The information I've acquired in recent years has sent me down many a dark path over lost forests, over-production of meat, mistreatment of cattle and other animals, over-fishing in our oceans and injustice on so many levels. I'd like instead to leave a list of some of the amazing charities and organisations, working around the clock to make our world a better place with a sustainable future.

The World Wide Fund for Nature (WWF) (wwf.org.uk)
Their mission is to "create a world where people and wildlife can thrive together."

Greenpeace International (greenpeace.com)
Greenpeace is a big supporter of ocean conservation and forest preservation as well as protecting endangered species and supporting the prevention of climate change.

The National Geographic Society (nationalgeographic.com)
You might have read their magazines or seen some of their TV documentaries. They provide a bird's eye view into why it's important to save the planet.

Friends of the Earth (friendsoftheearth.uk)
They describe themselves as "part of an international community, dedicated to protecting the natural world and the well-being of everyone in it".

The Royal Society for the Protection of Birds (rspb.org.uk)
This organisation recognises the plight of our planet, particularly our dwindling bird populations.

The Climate Coalition (theclimatecoalition.org)
The Climate Coalition describes itself as "the UK's largest group of people dedicated to action against climate change"

COMING SOON

BOOK 2
CLASH OF THE TOTEMS AND THE
CATASTROPHE OF CALLISTUS

Join Ellery in her second year at the Quinton Earth Science School – one by one, another friend goes mysteriously missing. Who will be taken next?

Prepare for adventure in the ultimate totem battle as the story concludes in CLASH OF THE TOTEMS and the Catastrophe of Callistus.

Sign up for my occasional newsletter and other new releases.

yonniegarber.com

ABOUT THE AUTHOR

Yonnie Garber is a foot doctor (podiatrist) turned word-charmer (author). Her attention has inevitably progressed from ailments of feet to where those feet tread.

An ardent member of the WWF she is passionate about increasing awareness of human impact on our environment.

As a mother of five and a grandmother of two, storytelling has always played a big part in her life, so Yonnie has combined both her passions to mix moral principles with epic tales of adventure.

She believes that a change is growing in people's minds and hearts, spreading rapidly towards a greater respect for the Earth, so that we may all create an optimistic future.

 Matador

For exclusive discounts on Matador titles,
sign up to our occasional newsletter at
troubador.co.uk/bookshop